They Called Me 'The W'

They Called Me 'The W'

I Was 'Mom' to 2000 Plus Sorority Girls

W. B. Devine

First Page Publications

12103 Merriman • Livonia, MI 48150
1-800-343-3034 • Fax (734) 525-4420
www.firstpagepublications.com

Library of Congress Cataloging-in-Publication Data

Devine, W. B.
    They called me "The W" : I was "mom" to 2000 plus
sorority girls / W.B. Devine.
    p. cm.
    ISBN 1928623409

    1. Greek letter societies--United States. 2. Women
college students--United States--Conduct of life.
3. Women--Education (Higher)--Social aspects--United
States. 4. Devine, W. B.   I. Title.

LJ34.D48 2004   378.1'9856'0973
                              QB133-2059

First Page Publications
12103 Merriman
Livonia, MI 48150
www.firstpagepublications.com

Dedication

I would like to dedicate this book to the thousands of outstanding young women who made my later years productive and exciting. To my family who supported me in this venture, and to my friends who encouraged me to continue writing when I doubted that it would ever be a book. And to my grandchildren, who contributed their own experiences with love for my sorority.

mrs. w

THE QUEEN MOTHER

Chapter 1

When people asked me what I did as House Director, I always wished that I had two lists to show them. One would be my official duties, as spelled out in my job contract. The other I would compose, and it would be a description of how my official duties actually translated into real life — how I *really* spent my time. My first responsibility was to the women who lived in the house — to make sure that they were all warm, comfortable, well fed, and safe in the chapter house. To that end, my official job description included the following criteria:

* Supervise the upkeep and management of the chapter house, its residents, and guests.

* Assist chapter officers in monitoring and enforcement of behavioral standards such as visitation hours and policies regarding social functions and other gatherings.

* Assist the chapter Finance Officer in preparing and maintaining accurate chapter accounting records and

budget. Examine for accuracy and submit all invoices to the Treasurer for expenses in running the house.

* Hire and supervise all personnel who work in the chapter house. Schedule and keep a record of hours for payment.

So, what did these responsibilities mean in practice? They translated into a never-ending list of daily duties.

I always had to be available when one of the members sought advice or had questions. I had to remind the girls and guests, again and again, to respect rules and regulations because I was responsible to the House Corporation to keep the house and furnishings in good order. I had to be on continual alert when the fraternity boys were out doing their mischief. I kept a record of each girl's personal history, parents' names and addresses, birthdays, allergies and special needs. I handed out keys in the fall, recorded their numbers, replaced broken or lost keys during the year, and replenished all keys during summer when necessary. I had to ensure that the burglar alarm was turned on each night, keep all doors from being left open, and keep track of the petty cash funds for vendors who demanded immediate payment for services.

I was to be a gracious hostess to all guests, making them feel comfortable at all times. I had to be available to assist in any way during Rush — to help relieve the stress of long hours and provide food or snacks for Final Desserts, along with any other help and support that might be requested.

It was also my job to order all of the food coming into the house from the many different sources. Besides ordering all our dairy, vegetables and fruit, bagels etc, there were always certain extra things that I shopped for personally every week. I had to make sure the kitchen was always restocked with cups, glasses, silverware, and small and large appliances. I kept laundry quarters, both for the girls and for the staff. Order had to be maintained in the parking lot, which meant keeping a record of cars that rightfully had a parking spot, keeping the driveway clear, and getting cars towed when unlawfully parked.

I filled out unemployment forms for staff while off for the summer months. It was my job to open the chapter house in the fall, and close it in the spring.

* * *

The story about my life as a House Mother / Director is very real, but parts of it will read like fiction. As some House Directors would agree, a lot of the events are hard to believe unless you have spent some time in their shoes. This is an honest relating of my experiences and my feelings about them. I hope it sheds some light on what we do and some appreciation for how many of us continue to fill this difficult, but rewarding, position.

Dear Mrs. W,

I hope you have the happiest birthday ever! Thank you so much for loving me so unconditionally - you are a true mother to me. I can't tell you how much I love living with you. I know I don't visit as often as I'd like, but it is a comforting thought to know that you are always under the same roof as me. I will miss you so much next year, but you can be guaranteed that I will be around plenty to harass you ☺. Thankyou, and I love you.

♡. amy

Chapter 2

Not all people go to college, and not all college students join the Greek System. But if you have a daughter, niece, granddaughter, great granddaughter, or a college friend now belonging to a sorority, my experiences over the last many years may be of interest to you.

My first encounter with sororities was when I attended Northern Teacher's College in Marquette, Michigan. I was Rushed by one of the national sororities but as I was very busy working to help with tuition, I did not join. So sorority life made little impression on my college life.

Forty some years later, after marriage, children (boys), and widowhood, and after twenty years in the advertising business, I was again introduced to the world of sororities by a close friend who was, at the time, a House Director at the University of Michigan. She was trying to persuade a friend of ours to look into the possibility of being a Director. At first I was only half listening and I sensed that there was little interest on our friend's part. But as I started paying attention, I realized that the job being described sounded very interesting to me.

I had retired the year before and found my leisure time difficult to handle. So I had taken an easy job, with little pay and suitable hours to fill my time. I soon realized, however, that I was working nights and weekends and didn't really have a social life. Upon thinking again about the sorority possibility, I decided to write a resume (which I hadn't done for twenty-five years) and submit it to the placement center at the university.

In less than a week I received a call from two sorority boards requesting an interview. The first was rather a small house that was building an addition to their current structure and hadn't had a Director for a year, as they were reforming and had only just returned to campus. During the interview we talked about my life and experience and what was required of the position. The first stipulation was that I would be expected to live in the house full time, hire the staff, organize meals, order the food, see to general maintenance, and be responsible to the Board and the parents for the health and welfare of approximately forty women.

One board member said, "I have to ask you a personal question…why in the world would you want to do this?" It took me back because her tone suggested that there was something difficult or offbeat about this position; but she laughed and assured me that she was referring to my living in a house filled with young girls, with all of the problems that young girls have, and she wondered if I was prepared to do this having only had experience with raising boys. So from the beginning, it was a challenge and very intriguing. After a few more questions and answers on both our parts, they informed me that they would be in touch. These were wonderful women, giving their free time and effort to running the houses on campus.

The second sorority house I interviewed was much larger and just a little more than I wanted to take on as a beginner. So when the first house was offered to me, I happily accepted. Therein started a new phase of my life as a Sorority Mother (now called Director).

This was late summer and I was told that the house was being enlarged and work was ongoing, but if I would like to see my quarters they would meet me there and we could go through the house. They assured me that it would be ready for move-in in September, but as yet there wasn't even a floor in my living room. As I hadn't any expectations, and hadn't seen other quarters, and I was excited about the whole thing, I decided to accept the position and signed a contract for the next eight months. That is the standard length of any House Director's contract, and there is no guarantee of an automatic offer of renewal.

When a few of the girls arrived with carloads of their belongings, they found me, along with the ladies of the board, taking a rest on the front porch. We had been cleaning up for a week after the carpenters and plumbers, trying to have everything ready. We had been scrubbing bathrooms, cleaning kitchen sinks, mopping floors, and doing anything that needed to be done. And we looked the part.

It's funny, because the ladies had been telling me that I should never let the girls see me with a broom or dustpan in my hands. I was supposed to be a lady of leisure and be there to oversee the house and direct the staff in their duties. This was a lovely thought, and of course their idea of how it should be; but unfortunately, that is not how it turned out to be.

Mrs. W —

Thank you for your wonderful hospitality and our meeting. You do a great job with the women and they appreciate you. Continued success with the chapter.

Love,
Bianca
Field Consultant

12/98

Mrs. W
I hope you have a wonderful break and holiday - you deserve a Break!!

You make a wonderful (House) Mom - and we appreciate you so much! It gets hard being away from our families and homes But you, and the comforting of this house make it easier...
Merry Christmas, ♡-
Jessica

Chapter 3

A little about my new quarters: the larger of my two rooms (plus bath) was planned as my bedroom. It had only one window, so it was gloomy unless the lights were on. The biggest drawback, however, was that the front stairway where the girls ran up and down at all hours of the day and night was directly above the corner where my bed was situated. They would clunk down almost to the bottom and jump the last few steps with a bang to the floor.

This was the old part of the house so the steps were creaky, and any noise in the middle of the night was like thunder. I would quickly put on my robe and run out to try to catch the guilty party, but usually she would have disappeared into her room.

One night I sat in the living room within sight of the stairs, with the lights off, and finally caught the jumper in action. Of course she apologized but did not quite remember not to do it again the next time. You have to be a good sleeper to live with that much commotion — and I never have been.

Finally I moved my bedroom across the hall into a room that was intended to be a very small sitting room, but was just large enough for a bed and desk. I had to go back and forth across the hall to use my bathroom but I was relieved of the stairway noise.

Unfortunately I soon discovered that a fraternity house just across the street had very loud and wild parties every weekend. Every time anyone went in or out of their house, the doors slammed and my bed shook. My experience with parties and drinking had begun. I had also learned that Thursday, Friday, and Saturday nights were party nights throughout the campus — fraternities giving the parties and the sorority women attending.

All of the neighbors had protested when our sorority opened because there already were three fraternity houses on the block, and they caused more noise and traffic than these people wanted. But at least the parties were mostly on weekends, not every night. The new location of my bed helped and a fairly peaceful time ensued.

Chapter 4

I moved into the house in August and had about a month to hire a staff. That meant finding a full-time cook, generally a cook's helper, a housekeeper, and usually a part-time maintenance person or, as they referred to them, a "houseman." In the advertising firm with which I was affiliated I was used to interviewing and supervising business or office personnel, but I had no idea what was expected of people in this line of work.

Never reluctant to try something new, however, I placed an ad in the local newspaper and set up interviews. This was the beginning of my education into the people who worked in the kitchens of sororities.

My first experience with a full time cook was a total disaster. This young man claimed experience and know-how and was the best storyteller I had ever met. He was a very personable young man, glib and willing, and seeing as I had to be ready to feed forty-some girls in a few short weeks, I hired him.

Great challenges were in store. Despite promises that it would be, the kitchen was not ready for the opening of school. The stove hadn't arrived and other parts of the kitchen weren't finished, so I had to find a restaurant in the vicinity that would feed all of us lunch and dinner until we could cook for ourselves.

Finally, a local eatery agreed to do this and every day we walked the three blocks for our meals. Our menu choices were limited but as we had no other option, everyone cooperated and made the best of the situation. A few times when the weather was favorable our new cook fixed fruit or veggies, or other easy-to-fix food, and we ate on the front or back porch or in the yard. I'm sure the neighbors and passers-by thought it strange, but as far as I could see we were doing fairly well.

The women were very cooperative and understanding. They came from all walks of life, and were all shapes and sizes — blondes and brunettes, shy and outgoing. They were so happy to have their house back on campus. They accepted me and made me feel comfortable.

After the cook, the housekeeper, and houseman were hired in November, the next hurdle was to hire "hashers," or busboys, who came in to help set up for meals, serve the food, and clean up the dishes and dining room. They were usually fraternity boys, either living in their houses or in apartments, who loved having their meals furnished. Five were hired and we were on our way.

After a few weeks of the cook and busboys working together, one of the busboys asked how well I knew the cook. I told him that all I knew about him was what he had told me. The busboy informed me that the cook was not a cook, was not a student, and didn't belong to any fraternity — as he had claimed. Also he had been banned from other houses. After some investigating, I discovered that he was known to travel the campus with his knapsack on his back, walk in and out of fraternity houses, and pretend to be a student. I was shocked and knew I should have checked at other houses before hiring him, but had been pressed for time. I made a mental note to be more thorough in the future.

A short time before this, I had noticed that the cook had

been taking food out to his car. When I approached him about it, he said it was his, and had only put it in our freezer to keep until he went home. When I confronted him about his lies, the cook answered, "Ok," and left — just like that. Obviously he was used to being fired and he probably just went to another campus with his stories. Had I been more experienced, I would have warned all of the other directors about him.

I had inherited a houseman when I took the job. He was very willing, but needed constant direction. Each time I approached him he would bow, and every time I asked or told him something, he would reach in his pocket, take out a small notebook and write down my request. That took considerable time — too much — but no matter how I handled the situation, it never changed. This man was perhaps in his forties, had been wounded in service and was slightly impaired, although at one time he had been a schoolteacher. He had little money and wore a piece of rope to tie his jacket closed. But since he was a willing worker, we managed.

He would put on a white apron and after we were seated for dinner he would appear by my table to see if anything was needed and again do his polite little bow. After I left that house for my current one, I would see him from time to time. He would still bow and say, "Hello." I ran into him one time in a store and he still had his jacket tied with a piece of rope and was still wearing, even in summer, high rubber shoes. I was very surprised when he told me that he was taking graduate courses at Eastern Michigan University and hoped to teach again. He had also been student teaching and said the students liked him. (He was a very likable man.)

* * *

So, I had a staff and started my new life with over forty women who liked me. We settled in to become a big happy family. However, we were still not out of the woods. Three months after opening, we found that when the toilets flushed, instead of cold water running in, hot steam was coming out and it was quite uncomfortable to sit. Somehow while finishing the plumbing, some of the pipes were mixed. But this was eventually taken care of. Another problem was solved.

The girls could go about the business of getting an education, and I could learn the basics of being a House Director.

Chapter 5

Expenses to run the house were high, and mortgages had to be paid, so in the summer while the girls were away, the house had to be rented out. This meant I would probably have to share the house with young men, noise, and little control. As much as I liked and admired the women and the board, by the end of the second year, I'd decided to look for another house where I could stay through the summer in peace.

I submitted my resignation and they said they hated to see me leave but gave me a wonderful recommendation and wished me well.

Once again, I updated my resume and sent it on to the proper people for placement. I had become acquainted with most of the other Directors by then and knew which houses were going to be looking for help. I knew of a much larger sorority which was interviewing, and since I had gained some confidence during the past two years and had the strong recommendation from my previous board, I knew I could handle the position. I drove by, and loved the house on sight.

It was a large brick house with white shutters, three floors, and shrubs around the front yard. It was located on a fairly quiet street off the sorority and fraternity drag. I thought if I was to live in that house, I would be very happy. I was interviewed during their lunchtime, and in attendance were the advisor of the girls, another member of the board, and the House Manager. We talked about my experience during the past two years, and my abilities in general. I was thrilled a week later to be offered the position. I very quickly accepted.

It was such a large house I decided to move in early in July in order to become familiar with it before the girls descended on me in the fall. My quarters were much larger than the previous house and very nicely decorated. I was totally happy. The cook, house-keeper and the houseman came with the job, most having been there for a number of years, so I was spared the agony of more ads in the newspaper.

The board had told me that keeping or changing personnel was of course up to me. As it turned out we all got along famously and apart from getting used to twice as many girls I felt very fortunate to be selected for this sorority.

In late August the women started to arrive. I watched them pull up with large vans, station wagons, and U-hauls, and wondered how they were going to incorporate all of the things they brought into their fairly small rooms. They also had to share that small space with one, two, or maybe three other girls. But these girls were amazing and, after all were settled in, it was clear that they knew how to utilize every inch of their space. We provided each girl with a desk, dresser, mirror, and lamps. If they needed extra room for their computers, TVs, stacked cartons, printers, books, clothes, etc., they were allowed to take out some of the furniture.

Believe me, when these tiny, slim women decided to move something, it went where they wanted it to go, before we knew what was happening. They were like a colony of industrious ants moving things from room to room and floor to floor. Nothing was too difficult for them when they wanted it done.

It took days however, before they were settled in and made the rooms theirs. Then it took another week to clear the halls of cartons, boxes, suitcases, garbage, and anything else they couldn't fit in or didn't want. Sometimes this was accomplished only after a threat to delay lunch until the mess was cleared.

The women in this second house were again from varied backgrounds, but as a group they did seem to expect more to be done for them. They were lovely, talented, and smart, but not always willing to share the responsibilities that go along with living with many other people — particularly cleaning up after themselves. We had maid service — but not personal maid service. Although it took a while to sink in, eventually they did realize that everyone needed to contribute to our house's maintenance and well being. And so we settled in for the year, and I felt ready to handle anything that would come along.

Happy B-day
Mrs. W
We Love U!

Chapter 6

My quarters in the new house were much larger and quite nice. My living room had two French doors facing the front, and two closets: one very large with four or five shelves. The other smaller closet had louvered doors.

Twice a year the members of the house had what was called a "date party" and for this occasion the girls invited the boys. They were bussed to some place in Detroit where they either bowled or danced, and where drinking became the theme of the party. That's why the busses. No one was supposed to drive on his or her own. I had come to dread these events because when they returned from their evening out, the house was indeed in jeopardy.

After one of those "date parties," I heard more racket than should have been coming from the upstairs. So I put on my robe, (it was three o'clock in the morning) and went to investigate.

Too many boys, making too much noise, resulted in my asking them to leave and I tried to return to sleep. Not being able to do this, I went into my living room and turned on my television. After about ten minutes, one of the louvered closet doors across the room opened by itself, and my immediate reaction was a fear that froze my body. My first thought was that an animal had somehow gotten in, as I saw something moving inside. When I recovered enough to be able to move, I wasted no time getting out of there.

Some of the girls were still up in the dining room discussing the party and upon finding out why I was so upset, they came back to my living room with me to see what was going on. By then a leg was protruding from the closet — a leg that belonged to the body of a young man who was out cold. Now he had to be a small person to fit into the closet in the first place, but in no way could he have put himself in there and also have managed to close the door. He was too drunk. So someone had to have planted this passed-out college boy in my closet. I didn't want to think someone did this to me deliberately, but having been a House Director for a few years at this point, nothing really surprised me.

The girls dragged him out and told me they would put him in a cab and send him home. I went back to bed and tried to forget about the whole thing. At lunch the next day, my housekeeper told me that she had seen a gentleman wandering around upstairs, and he hadn't seemed to know where he was. I asked her to describe him and sure enough it was the same young man who, in the telling of the story, became the "closet boy." What happened was the girls couldn't sober him up enough to put him in a cab, so they put him to bed in one of the empty dormers and forgot about him. I learned that he had been the date of one of the new pledges but hadn't been seen by her or anyone else since early in the evening of the party. I never did hear the particulars about him or how he had ended up in my closet. My guess is that the girls didn't really want me to know.

You can be sure that after that incident I locked my living room door each night. I do regret, however, not having called the police. When I think what could have happened to him that night: he could have died in there from alcohol poisoning, or he could have choked on his own vomit. I really didn't do the right thing. I read a week later that a young fraternity boy died on the couch at a sorority and it was frightening. I learned a good lesson that night and never hesitated to call the police thereafter.

Mrs. W:

We appreciate everything you do for us on a daily basis. You are our mom away from home and the last thing we want is for you not to love us as we love you. We know that there has been a few reasons for you to loose your faith in us, but know that we are taking care of it. We are striving to be better people inside & outside of the house and hope that you recognize it as we recognize all the things you do solely for us everyday.

Thank you for EVERYTHING!

We love, adore, & need you

Love, All your girls

Nov. 25, 1996

Dear Mrs W,

I thoroughly enjoyed my visit to Iota Chapter. The house is beautiful and your staff is superb. Everyone was friendly and helpful. Thank you. The chapter is extremely lucky to have you.

Sincerely,
Anne

Chapter 7

Filling housing staff positions was sometimes a nightmare. During a period when jobs were plentiful, and people had lots of choices, it became a game. I would advertise in the local and college papers and the calls would come in. There were people out there interested in the job, but not interested in working. One time I scheduled three interviews in one afternoon and not one showed up. Or they would come for an interview, be hired, and not show up on the first day of work.

This happened over and over until I figured out that these people were reporting to the unemployment office that they had tried to get jobs so their checks would keep coming. They had no intention of giving up those checks for work. Those that I did hire, out of desperation, didn't last too long. I had many strange experiences over the years with the people I hired and fired. Here are a few:

* * *

I'll call him Benny. He came with my second house and could not have been sweeter. He was willing to do anything for the house and the girls. He was a houseman during the week and cooked on weekends — and was good at both. However, since a young age he had been a drinker and was now into drugs. This was not apparent at first because he seemed under control. He was like a son to me; in fact he had gone to high school with my sons. The girls adored him; he would drop everything to fix their bicycles or cars or fix anything in their rooms. Most importantly, he was very trustworthy. That is a must when you hire a man to work in a sorority. He had to go up onto the floors where the bathrooms were, if the toilets were plugged or windows didn't work, etc., so the rule was that he must yell, "Man on the floor" when he had to be upstairs. This warned the girls so that they wouldn't run in or out of the bathrooms scantily clad.

Benny and I worked for six or seven years together with little trouble, but as the years went by his battle with alcohol and drugs took its toll. It became very bad and the odor of alcohol floated behind him wherever he was in the house. I tried everything I could, short of firing him, but somehow he really couldn't — or didn't want to — quit drinking. On his bad days, he would stand up real straight when talking to me, thinking he was presenting a sober stance. And he would back away from me because he knew that I was aware of his problems and could detect his condition just by being close. But he tried so hard to hide it, it really made me sad. Things that he repaired would work only temporarily, or would be done backwards and as time went on, he somehow damaged more than he fixed.

He would disappear for hours at a time and I would have to hunt through this huge house to find him. Or he would have to run home for a minute (he lived over the back fence) for cigarettes. Or he would have other excuses to leave.

Unfortunately, we lived next door to a restaurant where alcohol was served, and where he sometimes worked in the summer when our sorority house was closed. I called or made several trips over there to get him back to work. It seems strange that I continued to do that, but sober he was the best, and I kept hoping for a miracle to change his behavior. Things went from bad to worse and after many unfulfilled promises to change, he had to go. It broke my heart, but I had a house to run and I could no longer handle the frustration. Because he had been houseman here for so long and knew the house so well it was hard to replace him. So there started an adventure in replacements that was both frustrating and ridiculous.

* * *

A few times when I was looking for additional help, someone currently on staff had a friend or knew of someone who might work out. I learned later that this was not always a good idea.

I was looking for a new houseman, and I hired a young man who my cook recommended. Next to preparing the meals, my cook loved to talk. He was very bright and knew a little bit about a lot of things, so he would engage anyone who passed his kitchen in conversation and they eventually had to back away to leave. So it followed that the cook and the new houseman, being friends already, had a lot to discuss and I was continually walking through the kitchen area reminding Jack that the kitchen was not his area of work.

Sometimes his jobs were in the kitchen and if they talked then I never minded, but when they were standing around when there were other things to do, that drove me to distraction. When the term ended, I didn't hire him back.

* * *

One houseman came to me recommended by another House Director. He was older and retired, and he was not a friend of anyone in the house, so I gave him a try. He told me he could help me lower my gas bills and had worked in a heating plant. In fact, he said he had designed them. I was on cloud nine.

I very soon found out that he was all talk — he was on his own cloud somewhere, certainly not on earth. I shared him with another house during the week, we both agreed that we had been taken. I offered to let the other Director have him full time, of course, but neither of us wanted him.

He said the Navy and the Army were after him to work for them and told such stories that I began to doubt my abilities in judging people. To boost my sagging confidence, I told myself that you really couldn't tell in a short interview what that person would do on the job, and after all, he had come recommended. I promised myself that I would be much more careful in the future. Fortunately it was time to close for the summer so I just didn't hire him back.

* * *

So started another round of ads and calls and the interviews began once more.

The next caller sounded so great — also retired, and he was willing and wanting to work. I was elated, but cautious. He was a family man, retired, with a young son about eleven and another in his late teens. He was neat and gentle — didn't visit and did his work. Perfect. I couldn't believe my luck. He was happy and we were happy; I think he stayed with us for two years.

While he was still with us, I am so sorry to say, he developed pancreatic cancer and had to go through all of the surgeries and therapy. I kept the job open for him by hiring temporary help. He did come back eventually, but after one week realized he couldn't quite make it and had to give it up. He died shortly after that and I will not forget him. I think about his family and how they coped. I have such admiration for people who get through those tough times.

* * *

My next houseman was Ian. One of the women on our corporation board was shopping at the mall when she ran into my housekeeper, who happened to be chatting with Ian. The vacancy was mentioned, and Ian said he knew of a man who might be interested. Well it turned out that Ian was the man who was interested. After talking about it to me, he was hired and proved to be another treasure.

He was a very tall man and aimed to please in everything he did. He was very handy at fixing things and always in a cheerful mood. If you asked him how he was he would say, "Always good, always good," and he meant it. So it was wonderful to have him around. When he had work to do upstairs he would yell, "Man on the floor, man on the floor!" in a very loud voice and if I accompanied him would add, "and one lady."

I don't know whether I described all of the duties of the houseman, but he did all of the heavy mopping throughout the house, tended to all repairs, took care of recycling, did the yard work, and anything else that needed taken care of. One of his duties was to put the carloads of groceries away in freezers, refrigerators, or on shelves, and to keep the food storage rooms clean and orderly. If you can imagine the amounts of food delivered several times a week, you can see why he would shake his head in disbelief as he went about this task. He loved to laugh and he fit right in with the current staff. We worked hard but had fun doing it. The girls noticed this and it gave them a sense of being secure.

* * *

I had problems filling other positions on the staff as well — the assistant to the cook, for instance. When I advertised in the newspaper the ad usually read, "Cook's Assistant. Duties included: cutting all kinds of veggies for the salad bar, setting up for lunch, and cleaning up the dishes and tables after lunch, whatever it takes to make the kitchen ready for dinner preparation." When a new hire appeared for work in the capacity of helper, or assistant, they sometimes objected to the amount of work and quit.

One new hopeful showed up for work at 8:30 A.M. and at 9:00 A.M. was having her first smoke out in the back yard. Every half-hour after that the same thing occurred, but now the housekeeper was accompanying her. She had also just been hired, and the two hit it off.

After this happened three or four times during their first day on the job, I explained to them that this was unacceptable. They were expected to work and I had outlined their duties for them. They weren't too happy with me but I went about my other plans for the day.

I stopped by my office a half hour later and found two set of keys to the back door on my desk. Both had left without a word, and sad to say, it was not surprising. It was, however, very irritating.

My next experience was with a woman who spoke very little English, so her son accompanied her to the interview. I hired this woman because she was very neat and soft spoken and really seemed to want to be involved in our house. She tried very hard, and except for her strange ideas of cleaning, it worked for a while. Instead of using a bar towel, which we used by the dozen every day for cleaning, she used small pieces of paper towel to wash and dry counters, or whatever else she happened to be wiping down. We found tiny pieces of paper all over the kitchen.

During lunch one day, someone complained about the taste of the ranch dressing. After I tasted it, along with the cook, we discovered that she couldn't read the labels on the food jars and had mixed the wrong things in the dressing. It wasn't anything dangerous, but on thinking it over I realized that it could have been a disaster. Exit another cook's helper.

* * *

The next assistant was also allergic to work and could be found in the TV room watching with the girls. When confronted with the fact that she was supposed to be working, she seemed surprised. She was also found in my office, where she had no business, and asked the girls a lot of questions about the alarm system in the house and which doors were protected. End of another assistant.

* * *

The next cook's helper also spent too much time visiting. She was found several times watching TV during her working hours, and when confronted by me said, "OK fire me," which I promptly did.

* * *

My next experience was a very sad one with a young boy who had been badly burned. His face and eyes were terribly puckered and I knew he needed the job. It seemed that his family was all out of state and he was alone. He worked very well for a month, doing all of the things that had to be done and he seemed to like it. Then he arrived one morning drunk, cut his fingers on our sharp knives, and was bleeding all over the salad mixes.

I talked to him about his drinking and he was so sorry that I decided to give him one more chance. The drinking had happened several times at this point, and I told him that the next time he would have to go. I really tried to reason with him because of what had happened years ago with my other houseman, and I wanted to give him the benefit of the doubt. His next scheduled workday he didn't show up at all, and that was the end of another potentially good worker.

* * *

After so many disappointments, I finally resorted to an employment agency to find a cook's helper. This seemed ridiculous because the people I needed generally would not go through an agency because they would have to pay a fee. At any rate they did send me a woman to help the cook. She appeared for work on her first day with one-inch long fingernails ready to cut up veggies for the salad bar. I was shocked that an agency would send someone like that — she couldn't possibly put on rubber gloves, which is a requirement in our kitchen. So another potential was lost.

* * *

Things were getting pretty hectic with only one cook and over sixty girls, busboys, and staff to feed, so against my better judgment, I hired a friend of the current cook. I had tried to avoid this at any cost, but now I was at my wits' end. This one turned out to be a blessing as she proved to be an excellent worker, and though she and the cook visited a lot of the time, they did it while they worked and all was right in the kitchen once again. I offered up a silent prayer.

Now I had trouble keeping the housekeeper out of the kitchen where she also wanted to visit. It was certainly understandable because it sounded like they were having fun. After I explained that she couldn't get her work done and visit too, she heeded my warning. For a few days following our little talk she would answer any questions from me with, "Yes Ma'am" and "No Ma'am." Then things returned to normal. The new assistant stayed with us until family conditions warranted her leaving, and we were all sad to see her go. I tried to keep the conscientious workers but nothing is forever and you have to go from there.

* * *

The next helper was a friend of someone in my family and she was wonderful. So now we had two people in the kitchen who kept things humming and clean. Each time I walked through, they were either cutting, chopping, mixing, or wiping, and it was spotless. It sort of reminded me of my mother when I was young. She always had a dishcloth in her hand and everything was ultra clean in our house. But that could be another book.

* * *

I was fortunate to have the same housekeeper for many years and her job was not easy. Every day she emptied the trash in the bathrooms (which was plentiful), cleaned the wash bowls (generally full of hair, eyebrow pencil shavings, hardened toothpaste, etc.,), cleaned the toilets (which sometimes did not get flushed, or were plugged), mopped the bathroom floors and scoured the showers (which were used all hours of the day and night). It was also her job to keep the bathrooms supplied with toilet paper, paper towels, and other essentials for women.

During the course of a week we might have two plugged toilets, leaky facets, and a stopped-up shower stall — all making for very wet floors. She also dusted, vacuumed, and cleaned all of the public rooms, picking up after the girls. On any given day there were coats, books, keys, umbrellas, and knapsacks left in many rooms. We had sort of a lost and found area in our mailroom where we put all the stuff she had to pick up so that she could clean thoroughly.

Before the above-mentioned housekeeper, I had a wonderful woman who again spoke very little English but was very dedicated. She was here when I came to this house and was the one who made the wonderful graduate cakes for the seniors that I'll tell you about later. She came from Romania and was used to working hard. She appeared for work at 4:30 in the morning and left at noon, because that was the only time her family could drive her here and pick her up. She had ten children and after working her eight hours would return home to take care of her own house and family.

Her husband was a white-collar worker in Romania, but could only get menial jobs here, so everyone in the family had to work. Her daughters came with her from time to time to help with the heavy jobs in the house.

One morning very early, around five A.M., she slipped in the kitchen on an ice cube and hurt her knee. She continued to work with great pain and around six A.M., her daughter convinced her to wake me. I immediately called an ambulance to take her to the emergency room. She had broken her knee and because she had continued to walk on it the situation was very bad.

After they fixed her knee at the hospital they sent her home and before I could visit or talk to her, she had a stroke and died. I felt terrible, as we all did, and we expressed our sympathy to her family. One of her daughters came to see us later and I persuaded

her to take back gifts her mother had given to me, as a reminder
of her generous nature.

* * *

Some years, keeping a staff, or even finding one, was very
frustrating, but there were other times when, except for the
houseman, the same staff came back year after year and were all
happy with their jobs. The girls, of course, were affected by how
the staff worked together. They told me often that having a
happy staff — with plenty of visiting, humor, and laughing in the
kitchen — made the house feel more like a home to them.

THE CLOTHES LEFT ON
TOP OF THE DRYERS ARE
TURNING BROWN!
TOMORROW THEY WILL BE
BAGGED UP!!!

ALSO, PLEASE DON'T LEAVE
YOUR THINGS IN THE WASHERS
FOR DAYS!   tks
                    W.

Mrs. W.
    I just wanted to take a
second and apologize for
my friend making a mess in
the kitchen (the juice spilling
incident). He felt horrible
and I am sorry that I left
him unattended. I promise
that I will do my best to
prevent something like that
from happening again.
        Sincerely,
        Jenny

Chapter 8

I firmly believe that the houseman is worth his weight in gold. Throughout the years anything and everything had been glued, wired, nailed, replaced or thrown away. He was called upon to do all of these things besides his regular mopping, recycling, and outdoor work.

Doorknobs had to be replaced regularly — inside and outside doors, closets, and cupboards. Props that were installed on the bottom of the doors continually came off. Foreign objects were placed by the hinges to keep the doors open, which ended up springing the hinges and breaking the doors. For fire precaution, doors had to close properly and they frequently needed adjustment. At my insistence (even though it was against the rules) all of the bedroom doors had kerchiefs placed around the latches to reduce the noise of slamming.

Window latches and locks became loose or were broken or missing. Window handles had to be put back. Panes of glass had to be replaced and sometimes the wood around the panes themselves was broken. Each year we replaced several dozen curtain rods. There was nothing to keep the rods from expanding beyond the window and because the girls pushed their beds right up against the windows, the rods bent in the middle.

New and old machinery in the house created problems that either had to be handled immediately, or took hours or days.

Since the furnaces and boilers were very old, we had numerous flooded basements when the pumps broke down. Usually it happened in the middle of the night, like all surprising incidents, when it was a question of waking someone up or paying triple for services.

If I did call for maintenance and it was something that could have waited until morning, I felt rather guilty. But if the repairperson informed me that we would have been without hot water in the morning I was happy I chose to call. Then, of course, if I did call I had to wait up until they arrived, stay with them while they did what they had to do, and then try to get back to sleep when they left.

Can you imagine the hue and cry of the women in the morning when the showers couldn't produce hot water? One by one the complaints came down and there were no logical excuses for this mishap that could placate them. Sixty women taking cold showers is a hard thing to listen to. Even after the problem was taken care of, it sometimes took hours for the water to get hot again.

Rotor Rooter should have been part of our house. They were constantly dealing with various things that wouldn't go freely through the pipes. I won't mention the specific items, but it doesn't take too much imagination to figure it out. As happened with our vacuums, things went in that shouldn't have. Then again, sometimes tree roots were the culprits and that became an even bigger problem.

Washers and dryers are wonderful machines, if used properly. I always posted instructions just above them in full view, as many of the girls hadn't used them before. Instructions, however, like advice, are usually ignored. If a load was unevenly distributed the machine would stop. Instead of asking for help or reading the instructions, they would take out the dripping clothes and put them in the wash tubs thinking that would solve the problem. Finally they would come to me and we would fix it.

If the girls left a sock in the wash tub and it plugged the drain, water would flood the basement floor. Too big a load would start the machine smoking. At that time I was always brought on the scene and it was repairman time.

If the lint was not removed from the dryers after each load, they either didn't dry properly or the machines would smoke. We really needed a full time person to sit in the laundry room to keep the machines working properly, but of course that was not possible.

We had a small sink in the kitchen area where food was available at all times — but it wasn't a disposal sink. One of my famous signs was directly above the faucet, stating just that. But even so, we frequently had to dig down and pull out anything from green beans to chicken parts. By the time the sign had some effect on the women in the house, they were moving out and we had to start all over instructing about it.

Almost the same thing happened to the juice machine. There was a small tray under the three spouts to catch just the stray drops that didn't make it into the glass. But the girls often emptied all their undrunk juice along with ice into the tray. Of course, it overflowed. I tried a sign there also, but unless it was right at the point of pouring it wasn't seen, and if it was, then it got splashed on and was unreadable in a day. We needed some-one to stand there all day and instruct, but short of that we kept emptying and wiping. Once, I saw a young male guest hold a water bottle to the spout and let one third of the juice go into the bottle and the rest go on the floor. He would have gone on to fill the entire bottle if I hadn't been standing there to stop him.

A coffee machine was also available twenty-four hours, but usually the person responsible for closing the house each night turned off the burners at that time. If someone decided to make a pot of coffee after that time, it was usually left on and in the morning we would have a burned pot. We sometimes had two or three a week.

I have often witnessed the results of people not knowing how to use a coffee maker. They would make a pot on one burner, then turn on the wrong burner, or they would make a pot and not turn on any burners. Or they would make a partial pot, which meant the next person to use the machine would find too much water flowing out and have to run for another pot. It was a continual source of wonder for me.

The two pop machines were in constant need of attention. Not necessarily in the middle of the night — but when the quarters and dollars were put in and nothing came out, I was expected to fix it. I simply replaced their money and collected it the next time the pop man showed up. Sometimes broken frozen cans escaped and spilled on the floor. It was one more mechanical thing gone wrong.

Toasters and toaster ovens were always available, as were bagels and bread for toast. But they were not meant for some of the uses to which they were put. It did not work to put peanut butter or cheese on either bagels or bread and melt them in the toasters. There was a period when someone put chocolate and marshmallows on graham crackers and tried to make s'mores in the toasters; we had to replace the small appliances quite often. Other times bread was left unattended in the toasters and would burn and set off the fire alarm. Sometimes it was hours before the air was clear enough to reset the fire system.

Often, on nights when the girls were getting ready for parties, (and before the entire house was rewired one summer) the fuses kept blowing. Too many women using too many hair dryers, and curling irons, along with their music and lights, all at one time, caused an overload and we were constantly running from fuse box to fuse box to find the one blown. It's a good thing that I am a night person, because they didn't leave for their parties until nearly midnight. The great smell of shampoo, soap, and perfume lingered long after they left.

The phone system in the unlocked part of the house was constantly vandalized. Gum was once placed in the speaker part, the list of names and phone numbers was constantly torn or taken, and a few times the entire phone was pulled from the wall. Replacing this system wasn't done in a few days — we were weeks without it.

Our Xerox machine was another area of breakdowns, usually with paper glitches. We had a contract with them for repairs and they were constantly at our house. One person in the house was supposed to be responsible for keeping it in working order, but if that individual wasn't doing her job, we were often without its services.

I used the copier from time to time, and once, when I went down to make my copies I found the glass had been shattered. It looked like a heavy object had landed in the middle of the glass and it broke in long shards outward. I was told later that one of the women had jumped up to sit on the glass to take a photocopy of her bare bottom. I don't know how she wasn't cut up badly but was assured that she was ok. I don't even think I was shocked. Maybe a little surprised at the identity of the girl who did it, but not the event.

The company repairperson who kept our machines in working order wasn't in the least surprised. She had seen it before and asked if they were having sex on it. That did shock me a little. The girls in the house decided that the guilty person should pay and it cost her over three hundred dollars for her little stunt. I don't know, to this day, whether she was cut, but I believe the event had to have left some marks.

We had dining room tables with pedestals that were beautiful. Two each per table. Though these tables were lovely and expensive they didn't withstand wear and tear. I can't count the times I found girls sitting on the edge of the tables, causing the legs to break away from the glue. After that, we had wobbly tables. Or before I could intervene, they would be painting posters, sprinkling sparkling stuff, or cutting with Exacto knives on the tabletops. This was over and above the food and drinks that were spilled. So from time to time our tables were upended in the dining room and braced, glued or nailed, again and again, and we hoped that they would make it through another semester.

We had the large carpet areas cleaned by professionals several times during the year, but had our own cleaning device for in-between. The carpeting in the TV room and the dining room, although originally a plain color, sometimes looked like a flowered pattern. It was decorated with a mixture of ketchup, mustard, milk, spaghetti sauce, chocolate — anything on the menu — which resulted in the rug looking oriental. Maybe we should have bought oriental rugs to start with. Foreign matter from the outside was also tracked in, especially during moving in and moving out times. Food was dropped on the stairs while transporting it up to the rooms (even though it was not supposed to go there). Hot irons were left on carpets leaving burned areas (dangerous) and carpets had to be replaced.

Lamps and lampshades were always in danger. They were either moved, or the shades slanted for better light, or the bulbs were taken out for other purposes. Plugs were yanked out of the wall by the cord so we had bent prongs. Some lamps turned up missing. This happened mostly in the spring, the time when women were moving out to apartments. Sometimes mattresses, paper supplies, and other necessities would go also.

Furniture in the bedrooms really took a beating. When the

girls changed bedrooms in January, instead of moving their clothes, they moved the dresser drawers. This made moving less stressful for them, but left a very difficult time for Mr. Fixit. Somehow the tracks that the drawers had to slide on were just a little off and the drawer would either not close, or would drop down or wouldn't fit at all. Each dresser and desk was numbered at one time, so that all of the drawers matched their dressers and desks. These pieces of furniture were moved from floor to floor and in and out of closets and luggage rooms so you can imagine the work it was to reunite the drawers with their proper mates.

In the fall we had everything matched but you know by the time they stuffed too many things inside, the drawers didn't work anyhow. Too many things were jammed into the desk drawers and we were constantly fixing those. Clothes were mostly left on the floor anyway, so it was frustrating. One of my cooks suggested we furnish two large laundry baskets: one for clean, and one for dirty clothes. I thought that was a wonderful idea.

If a key was broken off or bent in the only door that had to stay off the alarm system, then of course that had to be taken care of immediately. That almost always happened either late at night or on a weekend when it cost twice as much to fix. But again, it had to be fixed.

Keys were constantly lost and someone would be at the front door, knocking to get in. They started with a very soft knock, then it was louder, and finally a little kicking would follow. As a last resort they would pick up the phone in the hall and call one of their sister's rooms to get someone to come down and let them in. I stopped answering the door about my eighth year, and I told the staff that they didn't have to do it either. The excuse from the girls was usually that the key was in their room and they couldn't find it. That was very easy to believe. Sometimes they didn't find it until they moved out. Some keys were bent in the lock and of course the entire thing had to be fixed. Definitely, keys were a problem.

Another job the houseman had, which wasn't exactly mending or fixing, was sweeping up the cigarette butts in the front, side, and back entrances. He put containers out for their disposal, but these became trashcans for paper cups, wrappers, food, or anything they had to throw away as they left the house. This problem increased as the weather became warm and instead of smoking on the back stairs, they headed for the outside areas. Then it would rain or snow and the butts in the cans (those that weren't thrown on the steps or sidewalks or just anywhere) would be a sloppy mess.

Another non-fixit job was to replenish the light bulbs that burned out or were at the mercy of the bulb snatchers. We had chandeliers in the dining room with candle shaped bulbs; we also had ceiling fixtures, wall and floor lamps, table lamps and tube types. That's a lot of busy work. Keeping a supply of all sorts of bulbs was one of my never ending jobs.

Dear Mrs. W –   2/9/99
    I just wanted to say thank you for
all that you have done for me while I've
been sick. I greatly appreciated the rides
to and from   the doctor's,
and the   fact that
you were   always,
and still   are

Checking to see how I'm feeling.
It really meant a lot to me!!
        Very, very much.

            ♡, Alana

Mrs. W,
    Happy Birthday!! I just
wanted to thank you for everything
you do for our house! Although many
of the girls might not realize it,
it is obvious that our house would
not function without you. Thanks for
giving structure to our house and
caring about our safety. Being the
mother of 63 girls is no easy task.
Ask my mom, she has had a hard
enough time with 2 girls! I just
want you to know we appreciate all
you do out of love for us. I can't
thank you enough. Hope you have a
wonderful birthday!!
                    Love, ♡
                    Mandy

Chapter 9

My day didn't stop at five P.M., like most jobs, but continued throughout much of the night. Actually it is in the middle of the night when a lot of the incidents happened. Incidents that were sometimes funny, sometimes scary, sometimes ridiculous, and sometimes just plain dumb. Most incidents that I had to deal with were executed by fraternity boys who were either carried away with alcohol or were made to do foolish things by their peers.

Many of the bigger problems happened at night (the middle of the night) when the fraternity boys were doing their mischief. Because our doors were locked at all times, and we had an alarm system, it was a great challenge for them to get into our house. Only the girls had keys so if they did get in I knew someone had to have let them in. We were rarely successful in finding out who opened the door.

Sometimes the boys actually did break in. Like the time three fraternity boys broke in through our dining room window, setting off the alarm, and causing many of us to run through the house looking for the intruder. We found one boy halfway through the window, but of course when we found him, he quickly ran away with the other two boys who were with him. So we phoned the police and described them and gave all of the information we had — including my age. (Why do the police always have to have that?) Then left as they always did and I thought that would be the end of it, as it usually is.

This time, however, it was different. Either those boys were drunk, or stupid, or both, because the police found them about three blocks away from our house still carrying our window screens. We threatened to press charges, but the president of their fraternity came over and begged us not to. It turned out the culprits were members of the swim team and would have been suspended from sports, and probably from school.

So I let them worry for about a week. I told them I would leave it up to the girls whether or not we would pursue this further and that I would abide by their decision. After another week, the girls decided to let them off with a promise not to bother us again. With new boys and new presidents each year in the fraternity we knew it was a short-term promise.

* * *

Another fraternity boy intrusion occurred once when a boy came to the front door and posed as a pizza man with the name of a woman in the house. The names of the girls were posted in the hall so this was no mystery. When whoever answered the door left to find that particular girl he and several of his buddies came in.

Mostly the boys wanted to take our composite, which had a picture of every girl in the sorority and was very large, maybe four feet by three feet, or larger. It was a tradition throughout the Greek system for the boys to take them. When I came to this house the composite hung in the foyer, right inside the front door. This proved to be too handy so I moved it into the TV room where it would be more difficult to take.

Somehow, and generally with the help of one or more of the girls, it still disappeared. Other houses built cabinets and placed the composite inside and kept it locked. The entire cabinet was often pulled off the wall, which required expensive repairs. The harder you made it for the boys, the more determined they were to get it. After we found out which fraternity had the composite, the girls were expected to go to their house and serenade them to get it back.

There was one year that it never did come back. Often it was returned broken, and if we could find out who had it we could charge them for the damage. I know that these composites cost thousands of dollars. If the girls knew they were fraternity boys we could generally trace it, but some of the thieves lived in apartments, making it very hard to locate them.

Of course the girls were not entirely innocent in this regard. They did their share of taking composites from fraternities, and then the procedure was reversed and the men came to serenade the women. A few of their songs were sweet, but usually they were about guzzling beer or being drunk. Everyone giggled and pretended it was great fun. My smile, if I was present, was a bit forced. Those were the times I tried to remember what it must be like to be their age. I tried very hard because I wanted them to have fun, but I didn't always succeed in understanding or condoning their actions.

The composites were new each year. A photographer would come for a few days and schedule each girl to sit for her picture. It consumed a lot of time and they wanted to look their best. After a few weeks we would get the composite back and it would be hung in place of the old one, hopefully to remain through the semester.

Mrs. W,

We sincerely apologize for our actions last night. We understand that it is important to respect the rules and that it is your job to enforce them. This disrespectful behavior will not happen again.

Again, we are very sorry.

Cori, Lauren & Elaine

Chapter 10

When many of the so-called pranks occurred, most of the staff had left for the day. They learned what happened during the night when they appeared for work the next morning. My house-man, who was a very tall man, could not believe some of the things he heard. His favorite expression when told about the incidents was, "Oh, sweet Jesus, help me!" And he would double over holding his head, while rocking back and forth.

These stories are funnier when being told than when they happened, believe me.

One afternoon before dinner I was coming out of my bed-room, which was adjacent to the mailroom, and spotted a young man crouched down in the corner by the drop box. He had his back to me and didn't move until I asked him what he was doing there. He stood up, looked discouraged at being caught, and answered, "It's a long story." I immediately suggested that I wanted to hear it and marched him into the dining room. I was going to sit with him and let him explain how he had gotten into the house and how long he had been hiding in our mailroom. But as we entered the dining room five or six girls seemed to recognize him, and with very negative comments about him personally, proceeded to show him the door.

I never did find out how he entered our house or his reason for being there. But finding a man inside, alone and unaccompanied, was not taken lightly. I again emphasized the need to always keep the doors closed at all times, and I posted another one of my famous signs: PLEASE DO NOT PROP OPEN THE DOORS.

* * *

The boys weren't the only ones to get into trouble, the girls got into plenty of mischief themselves. They had a refrigerator in the basement where they could keep food they ordered in. Or they could make a late plate and save things from dinner to eat later. Sometimes they put their name on the item and hoped it would be there when they had the time to eat it. There were always those in the house who thought that anything not tied down was up for grabs, and they would eat what wasn't theirs.

The girls started to put notes on their food threatening those who might be tempted. Some of the notes were amusing at first, but as they were ignored, the messages became a bit stronger. They started out saying, "Don't touch this" and signed their name. Then they added, "Eat this and you die." That didn't work either, so they added, "You don't want to eat this because I spit on it."

I had to take exception to that one and added a note of my own that said, "How vulgar can you get?" And of course added my "W", which was my signature in the house. By the way, the girls called me "THE W," not unkindly I must add. I know throughout the years there were girls who just plain didn't like me so maybe the "W" meant something else to them — like witch.

When the problem of food stealing became extreme, we decided to unplug the refrigerator, thereby eliminating the temptation.

Chapter 11

As with all old houses, the heating system was rather out-dated, and the girls complained a lot about being too cold or too hot. One girl in particular complained to me over and over about being too cold in her bedroom. After checking to make sure her storm windows were down and at least some of her furniture was a few inches away from the registers, I called a heating expert. They did what they always do — they told me that the girls' things were too close and covered every inch of the heating area, but they said it would be better. So I waited a few days and went to check for myself.

In the meantime her mother called me to say that her daughter was so cold that she was ill and had to go to the health center. She really read me the riot act and, before I could defend myself, told me that if I couldn't do my job maybe I should work somewhere else.

Of course the parents, like customers, were always right, so I said I would check it out again. I went back up to the room but that particular girl was absent, so I asked her roommate if it was warmer. She looked confused and asked me, "Why?" I explained about my little problem, and she said she couldn't understand why her roommate had complained since she spent almost every night at her boyfriend's house — all night — and was hardly ever in her room.

I had promised her mother I would call her back and let her know about the heat, and you know I had to bite my tongue because I wanted to tell her so badly where her daughter was sleeping, but of course I didn't.

Maybe her mother wouldn't have been shocked to hear where she slept. Moral standards and behavior, in my thinking, were very lax and I thought it reflected on the parents. One year, one of my very bright and popular girls told me that she had her own bed at one of the fraternities and very often slept there. She knew my feelings about the matter but, of course, it was not my business other than to express those feelings.

It would have been very easy to vent some of my frustration on that mother, because the hot and cold problems were an on-going thing. If the two roommates didn't agree on whether they liked the room hot or cold, they were constantly frustrated. And so was I, trying to please both.

When the girls complained of being cold, I would ask them if their storm windows were down. Often they said they didn't have any. In fact, usually the storm windows were pushed up to the top over the screen, but eighteen year old girls didn't have to know what storm windows were anyway did they? Each year, they were pushed up too far and got stuck, or they were not latched and fell down and broke, or they were taken out altogether and were lost. And each summer we had to rematch the screens and storms to the proper windows, replace the broken ones, and spend a lot of money on repairs. We could have explained to each girl about the ins and outs of storm windows and screens, but there just wasn't time, and to talk to them as a group was useless, as there were so many other important rules and regulations for them to remember.

One of our housemen just couldn't understand that concept. He thought all you had to do was tell them, and that would be the end of it. Since it never actually worked that way, he just shook his head in wonder.

Each day brought the sort of stressful events you would expect with that many people living in a single house — sharing bathrooms, sharing refrigerators, sharing televisions, and sharing closets. If there were five sinks in a bathroom, everyone would use the first one in the door, which rendered that particular sink useless in a matter of days — same with the toilets and showers. But then again, the sinks were abused if too much drinking went on and they were used to vomit in. We refused to clean some of those disgusting messes, so then they decided to use the showers for the same purpose, thinking that the spray would eliminate cleaning it up. It didn't work and although it wasn't fair, either our housekeeper or our houseman would have to do the dirty work.

Mrs. W—

Happy Valentines Day

Hope you feel better soon, we're all thinking about you. Thank you for being so wonderful to us, we love and appreciate you so much.

Love ♥ your girls.

Dear Mrs. W,

**Nothing fancy,
nothing fishy,
Just a
HAPPY
MOTHER'S DAY
wishy!**

Just thought I'd wish you a happy mom's day from all of your   "daughters." Thank you for all that you do for each and every one of us. We all appreciate your kindness and willingness to help always. Happy mom's day to our favorite House Mom!

Love, Sam

Chapter 12

On Saturday mornings, before the football games in the fall, it was sort of a tradition for the fraternity boys to come over, go up into the girl's bedrooms and wake them up for a pre-party. I was very uneasy about this particular activity and tried to ward off the men by meeting them at the door and discouraging them. I knew on several Saturday mornings the girls were very tired, as they had been up late during Rush.

On one particular Saturday morning, I saw the boys gathering outside and several were carrying paper bags. I had a feeling there was alcohol inside so I watched them closely. They finally came to the front door and were actually holding open bottles of vodka, and other alcohol. I flatly refused them entry. They had been drinking and I was determined they would not be allowed upstairs. They argued and defied me by saying they would get in another way.

I met them again at the back door where they were pretending to help one of the girls in with a large box. Again, I kept them out. They finally did get in through our patio doors. There were three of them. They pushed by me and started upstairs. I was looking up at one of the three and he looked seven feet tall. I grabbed his arm and he pulled away from me. So I followed them upstairs telling them I would call the police. The one I had tried to detain turned to me and right in my face said, "F... you."

I'm sure I didn't reply because I was speechless. But the threat of the cops changed their minds and they left. I was very angry and told the girls when they came down about it. They in turn informed the president of the fraternity and I hoped that would be the end to it.

Weeks later, I received a dozen roses and a letter of apology from the fraternity president, saying it would not happen again. Several weeks later, I heard that the particular boy had been put out of his fraternity and school. It wasn't solely what had happened at our house. He had been in trouble a lot and this was sort of the last straw.

I had tolerated the boys visiting in the bedrooms, as this was allowed, but could not see allowing them to enter when the women were sleeping. I questioned several girls about it and asked them what their fathers would think about it. They quickly admitted that their fathers wouldn't look kindly on it, so little by little the boys stopped coming around on Saturday mornings.

* * *

Another time after a date party, I heard a lot of noise in the kitchen and went out to investigate. The room was a mess and six or eight men and women were milling about. They were acting silly and actually staggering as some do when drinking. I stood there watching for a few minutes. Finally, one of the girls saw me and sheepishly said, "Hi, Mrs. W." One of the boys reeled around and said, "Who the f... is Mrs. W?" Again, that word that bothers me so much (being from an older generation). So I walked over to him, introduced myself, and told him to leave immediately. The women who were present avoided me for a few days — some apologies were forthcoming. I don't know why, but the boys they picked for their date parties were not always the best choices. I asked the women in the next assembly which rock they found some of them under. They laughed and knew what I meant.

* * *

Another time, during Rush at the fraternities, sometime during the night, the boys got in and turned everything in our kitchen upside down: chairs, tables, drawers, food in the refrigerator. They made the biggest mess ever. These activities were called pranks, but really, there was nothing funny about them when they were happening.

I really dreaded it when the pledges of the fraternities were turned loose and were supposed to perform certain weird acts. One time we found our garbage strewn on our doorsteps. Another, we found all of our doorknobs thick with peanut butter, including our car door handles. Another time, the hardware was missing from our front door — this was not ordinary hardware but very nice brass and very ornate. (We did get this back.)

Another time our dumpster, which is very large, was pushed into the very middle of our parking lot, restricting the movement of all the cars. Eggs had been thrown on the building and on the cars. Broken bottles were all over the parking lot. They had been thrown up against the brick walls.

Twice, the signs indicating where the staff parked were unbolted from the back fence and taken. Our next move was to stencil them right on the fence. Another time our Greek letters, done in a very elegant lettering, were taken from our front door. One time the front door itself was hanging by one hinge; they obviously couldn't get it completely off, so I guess we were lucky.

Very late another night I heard a crowd out in front and looked out our window. I saw a naked boy tied to a tree. A group of men were pouring beer all over him. Now this was not in midsummer and it was cold. I was told that the boy tied to the tree had just pinned a girl in the house. Now she was supposed to take a towel out to dry and rescue him.

I called and wrote to the Inter-fraternity Council many times to complain about the boys, but if we couldn't supply them with a name or the name of their group, there was nothing they could do. Another House Director and I even appeared before the fraternity presidents. We asked for some peace and the return of our property. And I requested that they not come around naked; we had seen it all. They were very kind and understanding, but somehow could not control their pledges when they were out to do mischief. I hope some day that this practice will be changed. I know I probably sound very intolerant, but after a number of years these pranks became very old.

* * *

I was so delighted when, one evening, a young man came to our door with a rose, which he presented to a woman in the house. Now that kind of behavior I could understand and appreciate. I wish I could write about more incidents like that, but sadly, they were pretty scarce.

If you are a
naked ---- pledge...
Our House Mom
does _not_ like Streaking
boys and [will] call the
[police]!
But thanks anyway
for stopping by

Chapter 13

Once around three in the morning, I was awakened by a lot of noise in the living room, even though my bedroom was quite a long way away. I quickly grabbed my robe and slippers and hurried out. As I walked through the door, there were about twelve or thirteen boys kneeling on the floor wearing dog collars, and one boy was standing up front cracking a whip.

It was a strange sight, but an even stranger one was in store. When they all stood up, except for the collars, they were completely naked. I was somewhat shocked, but having lived in the house for a number of years already, took it in stride and proceeded to chase them out. It was hard not to laugh because besides not being one bit embarrassed, they all crowded into the outer hall and asked me to come and help them get the door open. As the last boy was ushered out, he turned and asked me, "Are you sure we can't hang out here for a while?" Of course they had done a considerable amount of hanging out as it was, and I was glad to see the last of them, literally speaking, at least for the time.

Several girls who had been down studying were standing around watching but they didn't seem to be too bothered. In fact they seemed pretty amused and this actually bothered me some.

They told me later that they were more concerned with my reaction than theirs. I imagine they were thinking what their mothers or grandmothers would have done in the same situation.

It was not to be the last of the naked boys.

It happened again a few weeks later and this time the girls closed the doors leading to my rooms so I wouldn't be disturbed. I did hear them, however, and came to see what was going on. They had come again totally naked and were running upstairs and along the halls. Several were facing a glass partition that led to the bedrooms and were gyrating to the music in their heads. Usually drinking was involved so they really didn't need music I guess.

I chased them all from the third floor on down yelling at the same time, "I wish I knew each one of your mothers, I would call her and tell her how you were spending your time in school instead of studying." I was yelling and we were all running, and they just looked at me like I was from another planet. But they did leave.

Sometimes, if the girls were alert, the boys didn't get in. There was a window in the inside door so they could see who was out there. I never did find out where these boys left their clothes; they weren't carrying them. I did see one group run down the street after being thrown out, on an extremely cold winter night, and hoped the police would be driving by. Maybe the police did see them before they got back to their houses. But if I had called, by the time the police answered the call, the boys would have been long gone.

* * *

Some of these events with the fraternity boys were allowed; and if we knew who they were, and they were accompanied by an upper classman, and they took place at a reasonable hour, we didn't mind.

For example, one night about five or six boys were led in blind-folded, with heavy silver duct tape covering their entire faces. They looked very uncomfortable and embarrassed as they were made to sing little kids' songs, such as, 'I'm A Little Teapot,' while performing all of the gestures that I'm sure you remember. I have to admit, they looked totally innocent and vulnerable, and I felt sorry for them.

* * *

Around fraternity Rush time, I found a sign on the outside of the door coming into our house and it read as follows: IF YOU ARE NAKED PLEDGES...OUR HOUSE MOM DOES NOT LIKE STREAKING BOYS AND WILL CALL THE POLICE. BUT THANKS ANYWAY FOR STOPPING BY. This was very thoughtful of the girls and, in a nice way, without alienating their friends, they did the right thing. That year we had a few nearly naked boys but, miracle of miracles, they were all wearing shorts. Things were looking up.

But my hopes for permanent change were not to be. The next year they had their shorts with them, but not on. When I first heard the noise, I looked out my bedroom window and they were running across the lawn getting into cars, skipping on one leg while they tried quickly to get into their shorts. I went into the living room and the girls were standing around, not telling me anything, as I ran upstairs to find the ones still in the house. Two boys were just coming down from the third floor and had the decency as they saw me to cover themselves with their shorts. They actually apologized over and over to me as they left. They also kept announcing that they were from a certain fraternity. The girls knew otherwise. Not only were these young men doing obnoxious things, but they were blaming them on another fraternity.

I did call the fraternity they mentioned to let them know what was being done in their name, and was reassured that indeed they were not guilty, but in fact, they were fairly sure they knew who the streakers were. If they found out for sure, they would let me know. Whenever these events took place I couldn't report them because I couldn't supply any names. It was very frustrating.

* * *

It was tiresome when the boys came in naked, but it was much more difficult to accept when they took things from the house. They broke into my living room window one night and the only things I found missing were the clicker for my television and a small picture of two of my grandchildren. That was so senseless, what good would either of those things do them?

On Saturdays after the football games we had to be especially vigilant. We did at one time serve cider and donuts, and friends of the girls would drop by for a visit. So if someone strange came in, it wasn't noticed. One boy came to the door and as soon as it was opened several rushed in. Most everyone else had left, so they rushed through the downstairs rooms and took everything they could find and in two minutes were out again.

We figured that they were from out of town, maybe we beat their team that day, and we would never see the things again. They took a large, lovely fruit bowl filled with apples. Several jackets that were left on the chairs were gone. The top part only of my phone and a plaque from the wall in my office were missing. Pillows from the couches and a few smaller items were also gone. All senseless, as before, and there was nothing we could do.

Chapter 14

Busboys, or as they were called on the payroll records, "hashers," had been around almost as long as sororities. If meals were not served in the fraternity houses, the boys would find a sorority house where they worked for their meals. Essentially what they did was set up the dining room before meals, and clean up afterwards.

The set-up part entailed coming in a half hour before dinner, lighting and setting out the chafing dishes, putting place mats, water glasses, and ice pitchers on each table, and setting out the hot food when the cook indicated that it was ready to be served. Plates, napkins, and silverware were placed on a buffet table.

Cleaning up consisted of clearing all tables, putting the food away, washing dishes and pots and pans, cleaning the counters, and taking out the garbage. They also swept and mopped the kitchen floors.

One busboy usually set up and then ate his dinner. The ones who came later ate dinner and then did their part of the cleanup. It was a great arrangement when they did their jobs. Some groups, through the years, I could leave and know it would be done. Some, I had to stay around to keep play at a minimum.

The boys usually liked to work in houses that were close to

where they lived. That made it difficult for the houses further away to get help. So at one point the houses located blocks from the central campus area offered to pay them x amount an hour for their services. After that, we all had to follow suit and pay an hourly wage if we wanted to have busboys to help with meals.

One year, when my grandson was in high school and I couldn't find boys who could work on Sunday, he and three of his friends obtained work permits and worked both brunch and dinner each weekend. I can imagine how they loved telling their buddies about working in a sorority with so many beautiful girls. They did a little fooling around, but after a while were a great help and did a wonderful job. I missed them when their schedules were too heavy to allow them to return.

Most of the busboys I had through the years were decent, well-mannered, neat boys. However, as with anything else, a few rascals slipped in and we had a number of incidents that were not entirely happy ones.

I was very lucky during the years to always have enough busboys. Some would stay for several years, and when they graduated and left, would pass their jobs on to others in their fraternity houses. It worked very well, and if the boys leaving had been great workers and trustworthy, the ones they recommended were generally the same.

So, for my house, finding busboys was not a problem, but I learned not to hire friends of the girls in the house. Especially if they were dating. Temptation to visit was much too strong and the distraction too easy. I told those girls beforehand that if I hired any of their friends, between the hours of five and seven, their time belonged to me. Before and after that they were free to socialize.

The girls promised, of course, but I had to be continually alert and literally chase them out of the kitchen. They would think up every excuse in the world to talk to the boys — about school, about their problems, etc., but if they took up the boy's time then the work didn't get done and we were all in trouble. The girls knew immediately when I walked through the kitchen, they had to leave. If they knew I wasn't around, they would come back.

I chased one of the busboy's girlfriend out so many times I had to find another way. Finally I told her that if I found her in the kitchen one more time I would fire him. I'm sure he would have been unhappy with her because most of the boys need the extra money. It worked, and that particular problem was solved.

We had a smaller kitchen that we called the "busboys' kitchen" where the boys ate their meals. The women were not to eat with them and the busboys were not allowed to eat in the dining room with the girls. If that were allowed, dinner would not be cleaned up for hours while they visited. They all knew the rules before they started.

I walked into their kitchen one night during dinner and one of the girls was standing alongside of a busboy's chair, and he had his hand inside her skirt rubbing her leg. I knew that neither one of them thought much about that, but I had to admit I thought it carried things a little too far. I don't think they expected me to appear, but they didn't seem concerned that other people were present. Boy and girl relationships were so free and open, and intimacy had a totally different meaning for them than it had during my college days, but I couldn't condone that behavior.

I also observed that the girls were the aggressive ones. Most of the time the boys were content to go ahead with their work. They didn't seek out the women and were more inclined to keep the rules. Some began dating girls in the house and some became good friends.

Many boys worked for me for three or four years. They were very bright, hard working students and during their junior year were wined and dined by large corporations who were looking for new recruits. They had wonderful jobs waiting for them when they graduated. I wish I could have followed their careers. I did hear from a few, and when one group left they gave me a framed picture of them in their white coats standing in our dining room, with a lovely inscription which read: "Thank you for making your house our home." I'm sure they will go far in their particular fields.

DO NOT PROP THIS DOOR
OPEN WITH :
BRICKS, BOOKS, PENS, CHAIRS,
PACKAGES, BOXES, APPLES,
PAPER CUPS, PE RUGS,
ETC, ETC.....

ANYONE COULD WANDER
IN !!!   tks .W.

PLEASE DO NOT
USE THIS DOOR AFTER
11:00 PM .... YOU WILL
SET OFF THE ALARM.
                    tks
                      .W.

Chapter 15

I had become quite known for the signs that I posted in several obvious places in the house whenever I wanted either to request something or to complain. These were things that needed the girls' attention, but couldn't wait to be announced at their weekly chapter meeting.

The notes could be found on the refrigerator door (everyone opened that door daily, sometimes twice or more) or the outside of the cupboard doors where cups and glasses could be found. There was a bulletin board on the second floor landing, filled with information. Even though my sign might be lost in the maze, I tried them there too.

They might find them on the outside of their bedroom doors. Behind the buffet where the dessert was placed each night was another great place for my signs, or I might tape one down on the table in the TV room where the girls congregated for lunch. In other words I put my signs anywhere they might be noticed by a majority of the women in the house.

These signs measured anywhere between a 3 x 5 inch card to two to three feet, depending on the message I had to impart. I used white or colored cardboard on the larger ones and many assorted inks to be effective. Some I addressed as LADIES, some as GIRLS, some I just started out with the main theme. The one constant on every note was my signature on the bottom, which was "W".

I would never put up a sign either asking for or giving information without attaching my signature. It was very disturbing for me to find notes that the girls would put up without a name at the bottom. Sometimes the events that they were writing about had some connection with my schedule and I wouldn't know whom to contact about it. So that became another of my signs, asking for signatures on their notes. I have probably posted thousands of notes and signs over the years.

One subject I had to address repeatedly was the front door. I would beg the girls not to prop the front door open. After all, we lived right on campus and read constantly about people just wandering into both sorority and fraternity houses. My concern was for their safety. They would prop the door open with any or all of the following: bricks, books, pens, stools, twist the rug in front of the door to hold it open, and apples (we had a bowl of them on a table right near the door.) They used shoes, newspapers, incoming UPS boxes, and staplers. Anything on hand was at risk of being used to keep the door open. Sometimes they were just out on the front step smoking and didn't bother to take their keys with them (or couldn't find them). Other times they might be waiting for a boyfriend or had ordered food and were waiting for delivery. They had a million excuses for doing this and none of them justified doing so. Whenever I found something holding the door open, I closed it, no matter the reason.

I left notes: by the toasters and bagels about cleaning up their crumbs; on the bagel holder about closing the lid; on the bread wrappers to close them; over the sink warning that it was not a disposal; on the coffee maker to turn off the burners when they took the last cup of coffee; in the TV room to clean up after themselves, to take the dishes, etc., to the kitchen, and their personal belongings to their rooms.

In self-defense, in order to sleep at night, I posted signs to use another stairway after midnight and not pass my bedroom. I put notes on the front door as they were leaving to please not walk on the grass. If they subscribed to newspapers, to pick them up from the front walk and not leave them for our houseman. Signs were posted on the side and back doors, both of which were on the alarm system, reminding the girls that they were not to be used after eleven P.M. I put sign-up sheets for lunch and dinner guests. And I posted each week's menu on the side of the refrigerator. I also had a sheet for hours worked by the staff posted in the main kitchen.

There were many more besides these I've mentioned. It sounds like our house was peppered with notices, but remember it was a huge house so they were not that noticeable. Life was much easier and safer if the girls heeded my notes. I am sorry to say, though, that most of them were ignored. And a few were taken down by someone who didn't like them. I never found out who did this, but it was disrespectful to me so I let the standards committee deal with it. It stopped happening.

I'm sure the women were tired of my signs, but when the parents visited they told me they liked them. They at least knew that I was interested in keeping the house safe and clean for their daughters. These parents told me that their notes were ignored at home also, so what chance did I have? My hope was that some girls would finally realize that my notes were for their health and safety, and peer pressure would ensure that the rules were abided by. Peer pressure was one of the strongest forces in the house.

When they ignored my requests to stay off the grass I had my houseman put two stakes in the front yard with signs on them saying, "Stay off the grass." They were very roughly done, I have to admit, but I thought it might do the trick. My living room faced the area where they cut across so I could see them when they did it. But I was pleasantly surprised when one girl came to me and said, "Mrs. W. if I have everyone in the house sign a pledge that they will stay off the grass, can we take those awful signs down?" I was happy to oblige and they really kept their promise and used the sidewalks. Something worked. I wish it all had been that easy.

Chapter 16

At about five A.M. one morning I was awakened by pounding on the front door. A fraternity boy was standing there very worried-looking and said he had to go back upstairs to get his wallet. He had to drive a long distance and needed his driver's license. Could he please go back upstairs and get it? I reminded him that men were not allowed upstairs after four A.M. on weekends — it was against the rules. He pleaded with me so I asked him the girl's name. His next statement floored me — he said he didn't know her name but knew where her room was. Was I shocked because he had been with someone until early in the morning and didn't know her name? Only slightly.

So we went up to the room. A light was on and the door was slightly ajar. Music was playing but no one was inside. He pushed by me, went straight to the bed, raised the covers and pulled out his wallet. As he passed me going out, he showed me his license so that I would know it was his, and left. The young lady was not in her room, but of course she heard what had happened. She didn't look straight at me for a few days.

♡ HOUSEMOTHERS ♡

H is for hugs, we sure get a lot

O is for orders — like them or not

U is for up — all hours of the night

S is for sewing "Can you mend this real tight?"

E is for each student, whether short or tall

M is for mothering — one and all.

O is for opportunity to show love each day

T is for tolerance and patience, we pray

H is for housekeeping — cleaning up messes

E is for endurance, through all the distress.

R is for rooting for all teams at our school

S is for staying calm, collected and cool!

Chapter 17

I sometimes wished I could have been a House Mother in the mid 1900's. Over the years we have had many women come back for reunions — some who had lived in the house as far back as the 40's and 50's. They told me about the rules at that time. Everyone was in by eleven P.M. and the doors were locked. Dinner was always a formal affair with candles and everyone sitting down at the same time. No boys were allowed past the front door at first, then they were allowed into the public rooms only until a certain hour. There was even a small room that I was told was where the young women said goodnight to their dates. Needless to say that room is no longer used for that purpose.

I would have been much happier in that environment as I am a fairly quiet, conservative person. In my years in this business, things changed a great deal. The girls now had keys and one door was left entirely off the alarm system, so they could come and go all night. They didn't have to come home at all.

During my first few years in that house we had three sit-down dinners a week. On those evenings, the girls from one room (sometimes there were two or three) would come to my quarters around 5:15 P.M. and visit with me until it was time for dinner.

This was a wonderful way to get to know their names and become familiar with a few at a time. I used to ask each one to tell me something about herself that would ensure my remembering her when I met her again in the house.

It was fun and they enjoyed it. Then we would meet the rest of the girls who were waiting in the foyer and I would lead the way into the dining room. The girls who were lined up first had to sit at my table and then the rest of the tables were filled. (If they didn't want to sit with me, they simply didn't get in line first.)

Everyone stood behind her chair, the doors to the dining room were closed and they sang their grace. Each girl then pulled out the chair for her neighbor and all were seated. Because my table was first, the girls there were the first to select from the salad bar, and the other tables followed. The women at my table also brought me my salad and coffee, or whatever I preferred. All of the rest of the dinner was placed on each table so, other than the salad bar, no one had to get up.

After the doors were closed, if someone was late coming to dinner they had to present themselves to me and ask to be excused for their tardiness. Then they would be allowed to eat. In the same way, if anyone had to leave before I finished dinner, they also had to be excused.

On one of the three nights we had a candle light dinner, and the women were expected to dress. Nothing too formal, but no sweats or blue jeans or baseball caps. I loved those dinners and even though the noise of the voices and dishes was clamorous, I got to listen to all of the events of the previous night and something about their schoolwork and stresses.

After several years for some reason the women in the house objected to singing the grace. It seemed a shame to me but it was their house. After that they objected to dressing for the one dinner, and before we knew it, all three of the sit-down dinners turned into buffet meals. Some of their reasons were well taken: classes were being held in the evenings, labs took place late afternoons, and rather than have everyone coming in late or missing dinner altogether, the formal dinners were dropped.

* * *

The boys were allowed in the public rooms with no restrictions, and in their bedrooms until two in the morning on weeknights, and four on weekends. I thought these rules were much too lax, but they were handed to us from headquarters so we had to adhere to them. They thought that the girls were safer in their own rooms, with their dates, than they would be in a bar, car, or fraternity house. As we were not allowed to enter their bedrooms uninvited, they were on their own. When you mix boys and alcohol and privacy you invite trouble. There was a "no alcohol" rule in the sorority house, but we couldn't police them twenty four hours a day. I worried about it a great deal.

Mr. H—

Jessica is super ill. She is currently in her room (#18). She wanted me to wake you up this morning — but she'll wait for you to arise. Please see her — she wants to go to U.H.S. *immediately*

I have ~~no~~ class **all** ~~day~~ so — I cannot take her.

Thanks, Amy

Mrs. W,

You were a life saver today. It was so caring of you to "ambulance" 2 people to the hospital in one day. (especially after a loud + disturbing night). It makes me feel safe here knowing that you go out of your way to ensure our safety. I admire you for your kindness.

Thanks again,

Mandy :)

Chapter 18

To continue on with a few more adventures…

One afternoon, about four P.M., I went down to the house-man's shop where he kept his equipment to keep the house running. I didn't prop the door open with the stopper at the bottom, as I usually did, and the door closed behind me. I thought nothing of it, but as I was leaving the room the doorknob came off in my hand. While I stood there staring at it, I realized after a few seconds that panic was starting to take hold in my midsection. There was no other way out of that room. The one window was underground and had a metal grate over it. I tried to talk myself into remaining calm, found a broom, and started to pound on the door yelling for someone to come.

I knew that the cook had started dinner, and the kitchen was directly above, but he certainly couldn't hear me pounding, as the door was a heavy fire door. I continued to pound with the broom handle, and actually dented the metal door. My hands were becoming blistered. Ten, fifteen minutes must have passed as I tried not to start screaming from fear, and meanwhile looked around for something constructive to do. Obviously no one was going to hear me yell, so I continued to pound the door.

After twenty minutes had passed, I was really becoming frantic. Fortunately, we had two coke machines in that part of the basement. Two girls had come down to get refreshments, heard me, and let me out. Fortunately they could open the door from the outside.

I later found out that the cook, who had a drinking problem, had run next door to find his own refreshments. Even with a cake in the oven he was in no hurry to come back to work. But that is another chapter. Needless to say, I was shaken. I did suffer from panics, and that was too close for comfort.

Several years later, I received a phone call in my bedroom at eight A.M. and someone was asking to speak to my housekeeper. I had been asleep, so I put on my robe and started out to find her. As I tried to open the door, again the knob came off in my hand. I was locked in the room, and just for a second, the memory of that other time started the feeling of panic. However, I had a phone so called the kitchen and of course was immediately let out.

What stuck in my mind then was, "Would there be a third time? And what if I had been alone in the house during Thanksgiving, Christmas, or Spring Break?" During those times I sometimes didn't see or talk to anyone for days. All of the girls were gone, the staff was off, and most of my friends had families to be with. It could have been so much worse, though of course at the time it felt bad enough.

* * *

In our house, there were twenty-eight bedrooms, ten bath and shower rooms, living quarters for the House Director, and public rooms. Also a study room, computer and chapter rooms, bike room, storage, laundry, and furnace rooms. Being alone when it was empty could be pretty scary. We did have a burglar and fire alarm system, however, so eventually I became quite comfortable even when I was by myself.

There were house sounds that had to become familiar to me before I could stop listening to every little noise. During my first week in the house, I heard a strange knocking from time to time and couldn't quite pin it down. By the time I would locate it, the noise would stop. It took days to figure out that it was the ice machine periodically dropping ice cubes. Each night after that, before retiring, I would turn on a very old and noisy air conditioner and it would mask most other sounds for the night. With that steady drone, I could sleep.

I used the same method when the girls were in the house in order to drown out their noises. As they went from their bedrooms to the bathrooms, and in and out of the dormers, the doors were slammed all over upstairs. The doors had to close to comply with the fire laws. With over sixty women upstairs retiring at different times, movement never ended, and the door noises continued until three or four A.M.

* * *

My adventures continued when returning from the library one night while a big storm was in progress. As I approached the house, three fire trucks were out in front and many firemen were running around inside. We were required to keep a key in a locked box outside of the house so they could get in quickly in an emergency. My heart skipped a beat, wondering what I would find inside.

They quickly explained that a hot wire was down about a block away and all of the lights were out around the area. Our emergency lights had come on. However, after a short period of time they would go off and there would be total darkness.

The firemen did go through the house with me to turn off all of our electrical appliances, freezers, and refrigerators. I think we had nine freezers alone. I was left with some candles and flashlights, and because I read every night before retiring, I made do with the flashlight. For me, it was just another memorable night in the sorority.

* * *

Unlike all the other houses, we did have a burglar alarm system, and for that I was very thankful. However, with so many people in residence the alarm itself became a problem. There were certain rules to follow if the system was to work properly. Our alarm was turned on at eleven P.M. nightly. All windows and doors accessible from the ground and those on the upper flat roof could not be used after that time. All of our doors were locked at all times, and each woman was given a key at the beginning of the school year. However, one door was kept off the alarm system so they could come and go at any time, using their keys.

When classes started in the fall and the women were not yet used to the alarm system, they would forget and open their windows or take their trash out the wrong door, and, of course, set off the alarm. Believe me it was not fun to hear that in the middle of the night. I jumped inches off my bed and it took seconds to realize that it wasn't a bad dream as I ran out to turn it off and find the problem.

Then we had to determine who did what to set it off — was it someone in the house or was someone trying to break in? If the guilty party didn't admit their part in it, we were left wondering and had to check the entire house. So after we explained that we wouldn't yell at them if they admitted their mistakes, they usually did and it made everything easier.

It was very hard to get back to sleep after that happened, and it happened too often for comfort. Shortly after an alarm sounded, we received a phone call from the alarm company operators asking if we needed the police. If it was a false alarm, we had to give our name and password (a code that was known only by a few people in the house.) Unless we could provide that information, the police sent officers to check.

The fire alarm system was even louder and scarier. When that went off, the plan was that five chosen girls, trained to respond to the alarm, immediately came to the fire panel area. While I stayed by the phone to handle the call from the central alarm office, the girls went in search of the area indicated on our fire panel.

When all was searched and ok, we would tell the controller that there was no need for the fire trucks. If no one was available to answer the call when the alarm went off, or someone answering didn't know the code, they would send the trucks. Sometimes three trucks and an ambulance. It was always frightening hearing all that equipment coming down the street toward the house with horns blaring.

We had a lot of false alarms, which was embarrassing. The least thing could set it off: a bug crawling across the fixture, hair spray, candles, popcorn, smoking (though it was not allowed except in one area of the house), or even steam from the showers. The firemen were wonderful people and never got upset about coming out for nothing. They said they would rather come to a false alarm than a real fire anytime.

With so many false alarms the girls in the house would get very complacent and really ignore the signal. That was very dangerous, and we had drills to make sure they knew which route to take to leave the house. These rules were posted on each floor.

* * *

I will never forget one time after the fire alarm went off when the girls were checking the rooms, and I was by the phone. One of the girls came into my office with eyes as big as saucers, and kept repeating, "It's a fire, it's a fire, it's a fire." I had to shake her a little, and she finally showed me where it was. By the time we reached the third floor, one of the women had taken the fire extinguisher off the wall and had put out the flames.

What had happened was a halogen lamp had tipped over, caught the curtains on fire and then spread over the window and up to the ceiling before she could put it out. Except for the expense to the room, no one was hurt and we were thankful. The girl who had put it out was an outstanding woman in every way, with good common sense — something that is not always present in eighteen and nineteen year olds.

* * *

Another time when the burglar alarm went off in the middle of the night, a girl came running down the stairs to our appointed area. She said to me, "I think…" and before she could finish the sentence, she fell backwards and passed out. I tried to catch her but I was small and she was tall, and she slipped right out of my grasp and hit her head on my bedroom door.

We called the emergency crew and they checked her over but didn't take her to the hospital. It was thought that she had jumped up too fast and that had caused the faint. After a short while she was fine and it didn't happen again.

* * *

There was one more happening that I must include here. It started many years ago, at a local restaurant/bar establishment that catered to young people. Each time a customer celebrated their twenty-first birthday, there was a ceremony involved. A very large bell that hung from the ceiling was rung twenty-one times by the owner, while the birthday person drank a pitcher of beer. If they could do it by the time the bell stopped ringing that meant that somehow they were a mighty hero. Or maybe it meant that he or she had matured and could handle their alcohol. I'm not sure.

Somehow this practice invaded the sororities and fraternities and through the years changed somewhat. A pitcher of beer was replaced by twenty-one shots of alcohol or twenty-one glasses of beer. Although they didn't have to be consumed while the bell rang, the birthday person was expected to drink them all in a matter of hours. Since the place with the bell eventually closed, the ceremony was done in any bar in the campus area.

Imagine a young lady weighing one hundred pounds drinking twenty-one shots. You have a very sick individual.

During the year the special "bell" night was a dreaded affair for all House Directors. I have been called upstairs in the night and found girls lying on the floor, or over the toilet, or passed out in bed. Several had to be taken to the emergency room. Before each birthday girl started on this venture, they were provided with a partner in the house who was to see that they got safely home. And they were to see to them during the night. This worked until they became seriously ill and then I was called in.

Needless to say I found this tradition, if it could be called that, very upsetting and was completely relieved when it was over and no great emergency occurred. There was nothing I could do to put a stop to this craziness or I would have done so. We have all read of mostly young college boys dying from alcohol poisoning, and some women. Unfortunately, though, I'm sure the practice will continue long after I am gone.

* * *

It must be clear to the reader by now that the position of House Director was a twenty-four hour, seven days a week, all-inclusive kind of job. As the old saying goes, "There was never a dull moment."

Dear Ms. W,

This is just a little something to thank you for being so great the past two months. We love you being in our house, and truly appreciate all that you do for us.

Living here is really a pleasure.

We hope you enjoy this candy!

Thanks again and have a great and relaxing break!

Love,
Standards

Chapter 19

During the summer I usually stayed up rather late, as I was used to doing when the house was in full swing (it was easier than trying to sleep with all of the activity going on). After reading or watching TV for a while, I would fall asleep and wake up to a silence that was rather unnerving. The staff was no longer in and no one else was expected to come in, so I would take my time getting into the other parts of the house to check that all was well.

One time, on my routine rounds, I was stunned to see one of our composites sticking out one of the doors from the basement, half-way into the hall. I knew that when I retired for the night it hadn't been there, and it certainly was there now, so someone had to have come in between the time I went to bed and the present moment. This had never happened before when I was alone in the house and it was very upsetting.

I knew the alarm had been on all night, and certainly would have gone off if anyone had come in certain doors or windows in the house. I told several alumni who were working in the yard what had happened. We then toured the house trying to figure out where someone had entered and how they managed it without setting off the alarm.

There is a fire escape along one side of the house that leads to the roof and to a dormer where sixteen to eighteen girls sleep. The window/door, which has a push bar to open, was slightly ajar, and the lower storm window was raised slightly. Upon further inspection, we found that the storm window had been pushed open, allowing someone to unlock the door and come in. Another strange thing was that the alarm magnet, which would have set off a signal, was not making contact so they were extremely lucky to have used the one place that allowed them to enter without giving notice that they were there.

After further search, we found two additional composites were missing from the chapter room in the basement. They had also been into the food room because a box of crackers were found on the floor in the dining room. The third composite, the one I found first thing in the morning, was left behind for some unknown reason, maybe the thieves had gotten tired or nervous. I didn't find anything else had been disturbed in the house, but really felt strange to think that I was sleeping the whole time they were running around inside.

I called the police and they made their report, but there wasn't too much they could do after the fact. They found a few finger-prints on the window, but unless they finger printed every college boy in the city, they wouldn't be able to match them. And of course the police had to know my name and my age. I asked, as I had every time they came — and there were many times — why they had to have my age. They maintained that they could not make out their report until they had that information. So, of course, I had to tell them, but said that if it was reported in the newspaper, I would sue them. There was a small write-up a few days later and my age was not mentioned.

Like hundreds of break-ins, nothing ever came of the police report. If by chance they had to enter a fraternity, they might see our composites and then we could press charges. The policemen asked me if they did find them, would I indeed do that. I said I would in a heart beat. He seemed pleased with my answer and said most other House Mothers backed down on pressing charges. I would not. I had my fill of the foolish and crazy things that the boys had done in our house in the many years that I was in residence.

I called the alarm people and they came to reconnect the magnet and checked all of the others. I felt better about going to bed that night.

A few nights later, I found the bottom part of one of the storm doors half-way open and three of the brackets that held it in place were bent or missing. The inner door was safely bolted, but it was very unnerving to see these things happening over and over. I was fairly sure that the culprits were fraternity boys out to see what they could get into.

There was a restaurant/bar next door, and after ten o'clock each night they trailed past our house, some very drunk, and it was scary. We had four different bird feeders hanging outside of my living room window and after all four were destroyed, we didn't put up the fifth.

* * *

Most of the summers, however, were quiet and nothing happened day or night. Whenever anyone questioned why I stayed for so many years, I told them what another House Mother told me. "Where else could you live in a mansion, have your own apartment, have it cleaned for you, have your meals cooked, set out, and cleaned up afterwards, have your phone bills and health insurance paid, have a car allowance, and get paid besides?" Add to that: time off for Thanksgiving, Christmas, Spring Break, and summer too. It sounds like the gravy train, but remember the har-rowing experiences I have written about. Going to bed each night brought the expectation of "something's going to happen". Either the burglar alarm or the fire alarm, or some other nonsense would happen at any hour of the night, making good sleeping habits impossible. And that meant being tired the day after.

Chapter 20

One summer we had an incident that was very discouraging. When the new girls who move in as sophomores left school for the summer, the ones who lived out-of-state were allowed to store their belongings in our basement. So, in May, all of the boxes, trunks, plastic bags, TVs, computers, etc., were brought over and stored. Our chapter room was very large, and it was piled high with cartons for about thirty-five women who would move in the following fall.

After everyone left for the summer, workmen were scheduled to come in to replace worn carpeting, re-paper walls, paint, and do anything that needed to be taken care of. I happened to go into the basement one day to check on something and found the floor in two rooms and a hallway under about two inches of water. I was frantic — I knew the girls had very valuable things stored there and everything was probably ruined. There wasn't much I could do with that many cartons except to have them all moved to dry places.

The boxes that were piled on top fared better, but in a matter of days the smell told the story. I tried to rescue some of the wettest boxes and washed towels and bedding, but it was an endless job and I couldn't possibly do all of it. I notified the women and their families, and of course each one wanted to know how their individual things fared. I couldn't even move enough cartons to tell whose names were on them. It was a terrible mess. Finally, some carpet people came in with fans but the carpeting and pad had to be replaced.

Upon investigating what happened, I found that someone had taken a hose from the house next door to us, turned on the water, and shoved the hose down the stairs leading to the rooms in our basement where all of the things were stored, and it ran all night. Like all of the other foolish or malicious things that happened during my stay here, there were never any answers to why anyone would do such a thing. I'm sure they knew that the house was not occupied during the summer. That kind of behavior just didn't make sense.

A few of the women who lived close came and rescued their belongings before too much damage was incurred, but those who lived far away waited until they arrived in the fall to deal with the problem.

Just a note to let you know
how much I enjoyed meeting you
"Mom's Weekend". The house is
beautiful, the girls wonderful, and
you seem to make it all possible!
Again, many thanks for
providing a loving atmosphere
while Lyndsie is away from home.
Happy Spring Break! Fondly,
Linda

Chapter 21

In May, at the end of the semester, we held a celebration brunch for our seniors. Their parents were invited and it was both a happy and sad time for us and for them. They had lived protected in the sorority house, as best we could manage. Everything was done for them — good, nutritious, hot meals, a homey atmosphere, clean public rooms, etc., so it was scary for them to be going out into the world of jobs and competition, or to go on to graduate school.

One particular May, my housekeeper made two beautiful cakes for the senior brunch. She provided these out of the goodness of her heart and they were very special — all decorated beautifully with expensive chocolate and the best of ingredients. Our refrigerators were completely full in our locked kitchen with food for the next day, so we put the two cakes out into the girl's refrigerator with a note that said "Please, Do Not Touch," and that they were for the following day's activities.

I was busy in the dining room the day of the brunch when my houseman informed me that one of the cakes had been smashed all over the front hall (walls, carpets), and the other had disappeared altogether. I found out that a former busboy, who had a girlfriend in the house, had done it. As this happened after classes were over and this boy had left for the summer, there was nothing we could do. We quickly bought other cakes, but they couldn't compare, and I didn't know how I was going to tell my house-keeper what had happened. As she was not scheduled for work during the brunch, I decided not to tell her at all. I couldn't do it.

I was angry at such a senseless act, and once again was informed that alcohol was involved. But sometime during the summer, I received a note from this young man with a fifty dol-lar check. He apologized for his behavior and it somewhat restored my faith in the future generation — at least temporarily.

Mrs. W,
   I just wanted to let you know how much we all appreciate everything that you've done this week for passover. It makes it much easier to be away from home during the holiday!! I especially appreciate all that you do for me, considering I am a pain a lot of the time!! We all know how hard you work.
                    thanks for caring so much,
                         Meredith

IF YOU MOVE THE FURNITURE, PLEASE PUT IT BACK WHERE YOU FOUND IT.....

AND... DO NOT REMOVE THIS SIGN.
tks.   . W .

Chapter 22

There are so many aspects of living in a sorority house besides meshing with new personalities, new quarters, different food, harder studies, and the social life. Sleeping quarters were either a big plus, or minus, according to who you asked. In our house, only one girl slept in a room, so even if there were three dressers and desks, there was only one bed. Most of the women slept in what we called dormers. Each dormer accommodated about fourteen or sixteen people and contained some double bunks and some single beds.

One dormer was labeled the "cold" dormer, one the "warm" dormer, and the other was called the "early wake-up dormer." So the girls did have quite a few choices as to where they wanted to sleep. The women in each bedroom worked it out among themselves who would sleep in the room and who would bed down in the dormers. There were enough beds so all three in a bedroom could sleep in the dormers if they chose to.

They were not allowed to make noise, or have noisy clocks or radios and snooze alarms were banned completely in the dormers. They each had their own bedding, except for the mattress covers, and of course they brought their teddy bears or extra pillows so it would be like home. After a few weeks there would be signs on the outside of the doors demanding respect for others, especially requesting quiet and to please not use snoozers. They were very emphatic about their rules. When the girls themselves made the orders, they were more apt to keep them.

Peer pressure is very powerful.

I was not in on the sleeping arrangements, but I imagined that the women who studied late would choose to sleep in the bedrooms. That way they could stay up without keeping others awake.

This was the arrangement when I came to the house. Generally the dormers were full. However, one year, someone decided that they wanted to sleep two in the room, and before we knew it beds were taken out of the dormers and moved into the bedrooms, and what I called the "nesting" era had begun. For health reasons, I know there is supposed to be a certain amount of floor space for each occupant in a room, but I didn't realize what they were up to until it was too late. So we left the beds as they were for the year.

Then someone decided to put their beds up on cinder blocks to make more storage room underneath and there started (again before we were aware of it) the "cinder block" years. Now those blocks were extremely heavy, but when the women wanted something moved, it moved, and they carried them all upstairs. You have to realize there were three stairways in the house so I couldn't scan everything that went up or down.

Sometimes they took the frame off the bed and set the mattress on top of the blocks, sometimes they set the legs of the frame into the holes in the blocks, and sometimes they had two blocks under each leg. This blocked more heat if the beds were directly in front of the baseboard heaters because anything and everything was stuffed underneath. We also found that, because cinder blocks retain moisture, they were not being too kind to the carpets. To add to that, when they moved the beds around they usually bumped into the doors and gouged the woodwork.

We finally ended the "cinder block" era when over fifty of the blocks were not taken down after the girls left in the spring and it was left for our houseman to do. That was totally unfair because they were warned several times about leaving them. I think the final outcome was that each girl was charged so much a block if we had to remove them. And they were not allowed to reclaim them.

* * *

One of the dormers had an outside door that led to a flat roof where the women sunbathed for a few weeks in the spring and fall. Because the house did not have air conditioning, they would open that door to cool off the room and inevitably, each one would leave thinking someone else would close and lock it. This happened especially on party nights and when I couldn't set the alarm at eleven, I would have to travel to the third floor and close the door. It really frightened me because anyone could go up the fire escape and right into that dormer.

It was often in the newspapers about sororities and fraternities finding strangers wandering around in their houses. I preached and yelled about this constantly because after they all left for their parties I was usually alone in the house. But, like all of the other things I preached about, some girls remembered, and some didn't.

* * *

Speaking of yelling — one of the young girls was in the kitchen bare foot, which is against the health rules, (another rule) and when she knew that I noticed, she said, "I know, I forgot, please don't yell at me." I reminded her that I didn't actually yell, and she said, "Oh, I know, but you look." I had to laugh because I remember a look my mother had when something wasn't right, and I explained to the girl about that look of my mother's that had influenced me even after I had moved five hundred miles away from her.

I was told a few times that I had "quiet" authority. Maybe the look was responsible. I tried to curb it, but realized that with that, as with other things, I had become my mother.

Mrs. W:

I just wanted to say thank you for that new turkey (the smoked, round one). Everyone loved it! I really appreciate your thoughtfulness in purchasing it. You're the best!!

Love,
Linnea

Chapter 23

Almost every year we had people with eating disorders, and it seemed that they were the ones taking and eating other people's food. Locking or turning off the refrigerator affected the entire house. Many were inconvenienced because of a few.

Even when the food was safe in their refrigerator, we had problems. Food would be stored, maybe on a Monday, forgotten about, and after a week would smell up the entire area. Not only was that a mess to clean up for our staff, but a terrible waste of food. Six or eight late plate containers would be thrown out at a time. Girls were too busy and too forgetful.

It bothered me a lot to think of women taking things that didn't belong to them. And it didn't end with food. Some years, the girls would find things missing from the clothesline in the basement laundry room. Or missing from their dresser drawers. Or money from their desks. When you lived with two or three other women in one room, how would you know who did it?

It happened so often one year that the girls figured out who was stealing and set a trap for her. They even announced at dinner one evening that they had a hidden camera in the room and knew who it was. They were going to wait until the guilty party confessed. But the trap worked and that same afternoon she was out of the house with all of her belongings. There were some things the girls did not tolerate, even from their sisters.

BECAUSE THE
CEREAL CUPBOARD
WAS BROKEN INTO
THERE WILL BE
NO CEREAL FOR A
WEEK OR UNTIL
SOMEONE COMES
FORWARD . . . .

THE STANDARDS   . W .
COMMITTEE.

Chapter 24

Over the many years I was a House Mother, I learned something new each day, almost each minute. There were four phones in the house for incoming calls only. The dial had been removed to insure that no long-distance outgoing calls could be made. One phone was in the front hall, one in the TV room and one each in the closets on the second and third floors. We paid a flat fee for this service and it remained the same each month.

I was very surprised one month to find that the amount for one particular phone number was more than twice the usual amount. I immediately called the phone company (you could actually talk to a person then) and complained about it. She quickly checked it out and said that long distance calls had indeed been made from that number. I had to argue with her because, without a dial, how could you call out.

So she gave me the phone numbers that the calls were made to, and after some snooping around, I found that the girls were plugging their own phones into the jacks of the house phones and that way they didn't have to pay for their long distance calls. The girls admitted the calls and paid for them. I guess that is good old Yankee ingenuity, but I would never have thought of it.

* * *

In all of the events we had during the year that involve the whole house, the women were very willing to contribute their talents and time. And believe me, they had many talents. They did a wonderful job of planning and fixing, were right there on time to take part, and made timely suggestions.

However, when the event was over they all disappeared, and seemed to think that the mess just cleaned itself up. I learned during the years to secure the names of the committee responsible to clean, so at least I knew who should be doing it. Rather than hunt up six or seven girls I would sometimes do it myself or make sure we had others on the staff to stand by and help.

* * *

They got ahead of me sometimes, but I had learned through the years to anticipate how they thought. I particularly had to make sure that incoming girls didn't find out about the old tricks, because they had enough new ones of their own. Some of those tricks were passed down from the senior class, especially once with regard to our cereal cupboard.

We offered many varieties of cereals for breakfast; the cupboard was opened each morning at 7:30 A.M. and closed again at 10:30 A.M.. We did this so the women would eat lunch at 11:30, which was prepared for them by our cook. We paid her well to put out a great lunch, and if the girls just ate cereal, she would be insulted, and rightly so.

To get back to the tricks, I filled the cereal cupboard at night and the housekeeper opened it in the morning. That was on weekdays. On weekends, particularly Saturday morning, I opened the cupboard. One such Satudray, I noticed that half of the boxes and containers were already empty. This was puzzling as I had locked it directly after re-stocking, and had the only other key.

I finally realized that the door, although locked, could be pulled out quite a ways at the bottom; the lock being situated closer to the top. The cupboard was tall and narrow. So I posted a note on the door to the effect that there would be NO cereal, until I was told who was doing this. This happened in the fall so most of the girls were new to the house.

Finally, someone overheard girls talking during dinner, about how the seniors had told them how to break into the cereal cupboard without actually breaking the lock. Two girls admitted to doing this, but I knew there were more. So the mystery was solved, and the new lock was installed. I awaited the next surprise — knowing there would certainly be one.

* * *

After the rest of the staff had left for the day, many things would go wrong in the house, and if I could take care of it instead of calling in a professional, I would do so.

One evening, in my first house, I walked through the TV room with a plunger. Some of the girls were sitting in there, and one of them said, "Mrs. W, you shouldn't be doing that." I totally agreed, but stated that it had to be done and held out the plunger towards her. I was half joking, but she surprised me by taking it and actually doing the job. I knew some of the women didn't know what a plunger was or what it was for, but that particular girl did and was willing to help.

The same thing sort of happened once when the girls were coming in for dinner and I was shoveling off the front steps so no one would fall. A number of girls this time objected to me doing this so I handed them the shovel. It worked beautifully, but of course there were times when I was the only one around so whatever had to be done was done by me. I never really minded, but it shot my image of the 'lady of the house'.

* * *

There was another incident also, which made me feel like anything but the lady of the house. On my first morning in my first house, I awoke to find a note on my door from the current House Manager which was worded as follows: "Mrs. W. I was late for my class this morning because I had to stop and put out napkins and plates for breakfast. This is your job so please see to it that it is taken care of in the future."

I was shocked that an eighteen year old would write that to me and very anxious to talk to her about it. Unfortunately, after writing her note she went to classes for the rest of the day and I had to wait until late afternoon to see her. I called her in and asked her to read it aloud to me. She did, and when she had finished, she shrugged her shoulders to indicate she didn't have any idea why she was asked to do so. I said, "Doesn't this sound like I work for you, and my job here is to do your bidding?" She indicated that she didn't, so I told her I would check with the members of the House Corp. to see what their reaction would be. She didn't seem to care one way or another so I let it go and said we would talk later.

Because she was the House Manager, and as we had to work together often, things sort of smoothed out after she gave me a half-hearted apology.

Several months passed and, as I often have to do, I had a car towed from our parking lot. We had designated spots available for staff and for vendors who are making deliveries, so this was necessary. There was a strange, unlisted car parked in the lot. I inquired of the girls if they knew whose car it was before I called the tow truck but no one seemed to know.

It turned out that it belonged to my House Manager, and I was so sure she would think I was acting out of revenge. But she had matured in the few months in the house and very graciously admitted that she accepted the responsibility and didn't blame me for doing my job.

* * *

Most of the time I was acknowledged by each girl as I met them during the course of the day, with either 'Good morning' or 'Good Afternoon, Mrs. W, how are you?' This was done on a regular basis by some, but during finals when they were so stressed from studying, and most had come down with flu or upset stomachs, I would be met with glassy stares.

I tried during these times to make things nicer for them. I brought out snacks late in the evening, made sure they had juice and tea for coughs and sore throats, and kept the house as quiet as possible.

These same girls wrote the most beautiful and heart-felt notes of appreciation. I have a very large box filled with letters and cards that I read over occasionally or when I felt overstressed myself, and it made all of my efforts worthwhile. I almost think they were required to take a course in: "Notes for keeping our House Director Happy" because they all expressed the same feelings.

Mrs. W

Merry Christmas! I just wanted to take this opportunity to say thank you for all you do for us. Although we may not show it, we are very appreciative for all of the privileges you have given us. You have certainly made our house a home, which is more than I can say for the other sorority houses on campus. We are so lucky to have such a wise, generous, kind house mom to keep us in shape.

I will miss you next semester and next year... but will definitely be back to visit.

To wish you holiday happiness
As lasting and as true
As the happiness you always give
Just by being you!

❄

Have a
Wonderful Holiday

Have a very Merry Christmas, and thanks again.

Love,
Mary Ray

Chapter 25

The girls' bedrooms were their responsibility and we were not allowed to enter unless we had a reason. If there was a fire alarm, for instance, we had to enter to make sure all was well there. If I knocked on their door and was told to come in, then that was ok. Or if girls left their doors wide open during the day, I could observe what was going on. I must say here that these girls on the whole were much messier than my boys. It seemed to be the in-thing to throw clothes on chairs, or on the floor, or leave them hanging out of dresser drawers. In some cases you couldn't even see the carpet.

I asked some of the girls how they kept track of their own clothes. A few told me they could tell, and they knew exactly where their things were even though they were on the floor. Others said they wore each other's clothes so it didn't really matter. I was really shocked and appalled at the condition of some rooms but it wasn't my business to do anything about it, so I concentrated on other matters in the house.

* * *

One of the rooms, which was a quad, was named the *"love shack"* by someone years back, and it seemed whoever moved into that room felt they had to keep that reputation going. One year the occupants posted very pornographic images all over the outside of their door. I took exception to their taste in art, and told them if they wanted to look at it, to please put it on the inside. The rest of the house and the staff didn't really need to be exposed to it.

Another year the women in that room had so much junk inside, that six or eight feet outside of their door was covered with shoes, tee shirts, and other clothing items. I would ask them to please clear the halls so the housekeeper could vacuum, and I would remind them of the fire laws. They were always very pleasant about it but it just didn't get it done. So the housekeeper and I would throw everything back into their room. Weeks later it would happen again, but it was easier to toss things back than to harass them. I'm really not entirely sure they even knew we had tossed them back. How could they tell?

* * *

Trash built up in the bedrooms, and if it contained food or empty pop cans it would attract ants. Only then would they do something about the trash because they hated bugs. But if I saw trash in the hall outside of the rooms, I just kept putting it back until they finally took it to the dumpster.

Sometimes I think the girls figured we had room service. Plates, cups and glasses were put in the bathrooms instead of being brought down to the kitchen. Some were actually put on the floor outside of their room, hoping someone else would pick them up. Again, I had to threaten a late lunch, or no hot chocolate, or take away something that was important to them to make them be responsible.

* * *

House Directors had a lot of responsibility, but not much authority. We couldn't say, "If you don't do this, then you will face this consequence." Oh, I could do my thing about taking food away, but as soon as I threatened this, someone, and usually not the guilty party, took care of the situation and I had to relent. So we played these little games and some days, like some years, were better than others.

Dear •W•,

Thank you very much for the apologie letter. I'm afraid that I owe you one, too. I had a tough weekend last week. My Dad's aunt and uncle (my Great Uncle Frankie and Great Aunt Billie) passed away. So, that is why I didn't react so well. I'd been pretty upset and frustrated under the smiling facade I was putting on. But, you are right. I definitely see your point. From now on if I have more than 5 guests, I'll come talk to you. Deal?

Love, Erin

P.S. I hear that your Birthday is on Monday! :)

Chapter 26

The opening of the house in the fall of 2001 was probably the worst I experienced in my many years as House Director.

It started in July when I stopped by the house to check the food room and basement, as I did from time to time. I found that one of the recently purchased freezers was not working and everything that was stored in it had to be disposed of. The repair people came in the fall, as we are closed in the summer, so there was no hurry.

The repairman listed to my houseman and to me a series of things that could have gone wrong — one being that a connection at the top had come loose because of vibration, so the freezer needed new parts. It was fixed, checked several times, and forgotten.

Within two days, our double refrigerator in the main kitchen was making beeping noises, leaking, and forming ice on the inside. Someone came to fix it. In fact they came three times in one week, working right in the middle of the kitchen where the cooks were trying to prepare food and do their work.

While this man was standing on our steel tables working on his job, our dishwasher started to give my houseman shocks and so we had another service man working in that part of the kitchen, holding up the dish washing. When that service man left, another leak occurred and he had to return. The man working on the refrigerator also had to come back, because after several days of trying to make it work, it was determined that it needed a new generator. This would have to be ordered and installed later.

Two other machines in another kitchen, the juice machine and the coffee maker, both leaked and were not working as they should. Twice a repairman came for the coffee maker, and we received a new juice machine that turned out to be worse than the one we had.

On top of that, a leak occurred under the sink and spilled out on to the floor, which required a container to catch the water. A plumbing company that had been working on pipes in the basement returned, at my request, and fixed the leak under the sink.

During that same time a leak in the roof caused the fire alarm unit in the ceiling of a closet upstairs, to set off the alarm and the fire trucks arrived. Because we could not re-set the fire alarm until the leak was fixed, we had to have the roofers in to do their thing before we could again have full fire alarm service in the house.

Back to the refrigerator that needed a new generator, I had to check with someone on the Corporation Board as to whether we should invest money for the above, or buy a new refrigerator. The decision was left to me and I opted to fix the one we had. It would have taken a week to compare prices on a new one, have it delivered, and have the old one taken out. That was just too long to be without refrigeration.

When the repairperson was finished fixing the dishwasher he stated that we should really change all of the gaskets before they went bad one at a time. So he gave me a quote, which I passed on to the Board and was given a go-ahead on that.

While all this was going on the girls were preparing for and starting the Rush season. It is a very hectic time for all concerned. The meal schedules are all changed to accommodate the Greek system, different food has to be ordered, and the furniture is moved from most of the rooms to make room for the hundreds of women who come through.

Add to that, the hours worked had to be turned in so the staff could be paid. Bills had to be approved and paid. Girls had to be reminded to please not leave the doors open for anyone to come in, to keep the rules about wearing shoes in the dining rooms, to learn to park their cars in the proper spots in the lot, even though it was currently overloaded with service people's vans, and generally to learn how to get along with one another in this new environment.

During this same week, a few of the new women decided that they weren't too happy in the house, and one who had moved out was very unhappy out of the house. Dealing with such problems takes a lot of time.

One morning during this week, I was awakened by a mother of one of the girls who had received a threatening phone call in the middle of the night on her daughter's cell phone. Could I please go to her room and see if she was ok? Her mother had called her room with no result, so I had to find her in one of the three dormers. Seeing as there are sixteen or seventeen beds per dormer, I guess we should have had some system of knowing which girls slept in which beds. I woke one girl and she told me the missing girl's bed was next to hers — but the bed was empty. I went back down to report to the mother on the phone and she asked me to check with the roommates. Eventually one of them called the mother back to tell her that the missing girl never did come in for the night and had spent it with a girlfriend. Obviously, someone had taken her cell phone, made some calls — probably a prank by someone intoxicated — and frightened the mother very much. It all came out ok, but the whole thing took several hours of the very early morning to straighten out.

On top of all this, the paychecks that were due on Friday from Texas were delayed and a frantic phone call had to be made to make it possible to pay the staff on time. By the time we realized that the checks were not here, the treasurer in the house had left for classes and was gone most of the day. Most of the workers had left for home and now would have to make a special trip back to receive their checks. This doesn't make for happy people.

Shortly after Rush took place in the fall there was an event that all House Directors dreaded. It was a football game between two sororities and was played in the mud. I mean this was man-made mud: fire trucks came and poured water next to a fraternity house where the side yard was shaped like a bowl and that's where the competitions took place.

Through the years it was considered quite an honor to be chosen by this particular fraternity to play in this mud bowl. So much so that the sorority girls would wine and dine the boys for weeks in hopes of influencing their decisions. Each year they went a little further to please the boys and eventually some of the houses got into trouble by sending them cases of whiskey. I wouldn't be too surprised to find that the women offered more personal rewards, just to be chosen. At any rate, this kind of competition led to the Greeks changing the rules, and pre-games were played to determine the winners.

This was one of the biggest changes I had seen for the better in many years. In my opinion the nice rituals were dropped through the years, and the troublesome ones were kept.

So after the two top teams were established, the mud bowl was scheduled for a Sunday morning and usually during parents' weekend at the University. Which meant the fathers and mothers watched their daughters slide around in the mud. We had some very tall, strong women and they really played rough. One year it was a broken nose, another a lot of scratches, and many sore bodies the next day.

When it was over, I met them in our back yard with a hose and wouldn't let them in until the mud was washed off. Of course it penetrated their T-shirts, and right down to their underwear, so most of it had to come off before they were clean enough to go up to the showers. It was usually very cold, so they stood in line shivering until their turn at the hose.

So the shoes, pants, shirts, etc., were taken off outside and left until they could be rinsed and put into the washers. A few of the girls retrieved their belongings and hosed them off before taking them to the laundry. Some (unknown to us) threw them in the washers, mud and all, and the rest were thrown in the dumpster after staying on the ground for a few weeks. For days we had to run water through the washers to get rid of the mud. So for an event that lasted only for an hour, we dealt with the consequences for weeks. I know each House Mother hoped that her girls were not football players. I did, and I would not go to watch them play. A few times they brought back a video of the match and I did watch it, but it certainly was not one of my favorite times of the year.

I remind you that the events in the last few pages all took place in about a week's time, and some of it during Rush. All of it though was trivialized and felt very unimportant when, on September Eleventh, we were all shocked and horrified by the events taking place in New York and Washington.

Several women in the house were from New York and for the entire morning calls were being made to see if families were ok. One father was supposed to be on one of the hijacked planes but had taken it the day before. Another of our girls who had graduated and left the house worked on the 103 floor of the tower but had overslept that morning. These small miracles continued to be revealed in all areas as people talked to friends and relatives. I can't go into the feelings about this because it is beyond words. But it did take the seriousness from all of the problems mentioned above.

Thank you so much
for coming to sing
and variety last
night! It was so
nice to have your
support, we all
appreciate it so much!
Love,
Sing & Variety girls

*your thoughtfulness
is a work of heart.*

thank you

Lindsey
Heather
Julia
Lauren
Meghan
Lauren
Emma
Robyn
Maureen
Anna
Jenna
Tara
Jenny
Josie
Danielle
Anne
Tessa
Veronica
lauren
Lisa
Jessica
Joanna

Chapter 27

I certainly don't want to dwell on only the strange and frustrating happenings during the years, because many wonderful things took place all done completely by the students.

Greek Week was one of the most exciting and busy times of the year. This occurred toward the end of the semester and all sororities and fraternities took part. It lasted for about a week and a half during which time each sorority would team up with one or two fraternities to become a team. Each team was given a number and kept that same number throughout the entire time.

Different activities were planned for each day and any or all of the men and women who were free to participate would show up and compete. Some of the events were as follows: Tug-o-war, volley ball, mattress races, jello jumps, blood drive, anchor splash, golf tournament, lip jam, licorice chomp, pie eating, bouncy boxing, rugby, soccer shootout, and family feud, to name a few.

Each house also displayed a very large banner from the front of their house depicting a central theme, and these were judged for first, second and third place.

The final event at the end of the week was *Variety Night*. For several weeks teams prepared for this competition. Some teams selected songs and those groups entered into the singing part of the night. Usually a woman on the team would have some experience in voice and would coach everyone to do their best with their selection. They would practice many afternoon and evening hours in our living room, in hopes of being chosen among the ten finalists.

Similarly, the women who were into dance would choreograph and teach their team a routine. The dance teams did not have to try out as they allowed all teams to perform in the dance. I was constantly amazed each year at the talent presented on stage. This event was held at a very large auditorium, and when it was filled with all of the sororities and fraternities and they were all shouting for their teams, you had to block your ears. Besides, on each side of the stage were situated huge speakers used for the performance. Music was loud, excitement was high, and this went on for many hours.

All of the House Directors were invited and had special reserved seats down in front. Some years we were acknowledged and asked to stand and it was nice to be included and appreciated. The judges were also seated nearby. Some were from the university and others were professional artists and musicians invited to take part.

Each group presented their song, some with accompaniment, some not. Some were in costume, some added gestures. But all groups were generally very good. Next came the dancers, and each group performed their chosen routine. Their performances were always surprising and wonderful. Boys that usually looked awkward and clumsy were transformed on stage and looked wonderful. One of my busboys (shy beyond words, quiet, and very sweet) really surprised me when I watched him on stage doing these sexy moves. You never can tell, can you? We teased him a lot, and he blushed and was his shy self again. He was always a delight to have around and we were so proud of him. Two other busboys were in a modern dance class, so my cook and I went to their recital. When they were in my kitchen scrubbing pans it was hard to imagine them in dance class, but again, they did very well and they were happy that we went. The girls, of course, were wonderful. Many of them were in the dance department and were trained in ballet, jazz, etc. They always amazed us.

So after all of this was over, it was time for the judges to make their selections for that year's winners. While waiting for these results usually a film was shown of all of the events I mentioned above. Of course each time the students recognized themselves on the screen, there were screams and whistling and the noise continued non-stop.

Finally, the judges were ready and announcements were made starting with number five and down to number one, the big winner. The singing results were first and then the dance. As they were announced, the roar of those winners was deafening and someone would run up onto the stage and accept the trophy. When they got to number one, it was impossible to even hear the team number. And of course the House Director with the most wins for her house was cheering also and feeling a little superior. I have to say that after that night I, for one, was always exhausted.

It was a wonderful evening and during my many years as House Director I did not miss a single performance. I loved every minute of it. Back at the house, talk would go on for hours about the teams — who should have won, and how exciting it was to win the trophy. Then they all left to attend parties.

Dear Mrs. W,
On behalf of the Standards Committee,
we would like to thank you for
cleaning and preparing the apartment.
It is a great atmosphere to hold our
meetings in there and now all of our
guests will be comfortable too. We appreciate
you taking the time and effort.
Joanna
Andrea   Sincerely,
     Jessica Stephanie   Lisa
              Jill   and Jennifer

2-8-09

Mrs. W,
we just want you to know how much
we appreciate having you here with us.
we know we can be a little loud and
messy sometimes and do a number on
the vacuum cleaners, but we just
want you to know that we care. Thank
you so much for everything that you do!

we wish you a very Happy Holiday
and a safe and Happy New Year!

Love,
The Sisters

Chapter 28

In my sorority the rules were decreed by the National Organization. Within the sorority, the Standards Committee enforced the rules. This committee consisted of five officers elected by the members, as follows:

President:

The collegiate chapter president is the official representative and spokesperson for the chapter to the Fraternity, the local campus and the local community. She serves as the leader of the chapter by presiding at formal chapter meetings and chapter rituals. She also adheres to all policies and serves as a role model for all chapter members.

Vice President of Chapter Development:

She leads the chapter to realize the purpose of the chapter. She is the leader of the standards committee and serves to make chapter members aware of standards and policies. She leads the effort to recognize those members who exemplify the ideals, and she is responsible for holding members accountable for their actions.

Academic Development Chairman:

She is responsible for maintaining chapter excellence in scholarship and assisting members who are in need of additional academic support. In addition, she serves as the primary chapter officer contact for the chapter's faculty advisor.

New Member Development Chairman:

She facilitates the personal growth and development of chapter members by electing the areas of focus for each open meeting and planning the method that will best address that area of focus. She analyzes chapter trends and seeks ways to promote trends and further develop the chapter's areas of need. She is a model of personal development while exemplifying growth in the areas of character, unselfish leadership, intellectual life, and friendship.

New Member Educator:

The new member educator is responsible for preparing all new members for initiation. She plans and implements a new member education program that meets the chapter's schedule and timeline for initiation. Her overall aim is to insure that new members understand their rights and responsibilities and that they are able to live up to the pledge that they make to the organization.

These five women were considered leaders in the house and ruled on events happening while in office. With the cooperation of the House Director, they handled all discipline problems, eating disorders, and disruptive behavior. They met once a week, either before or after the regular chapter meeting. All members attended chapter meetings unless excused by the Standards Committee.

Other officers included:

House Manager, who worked directly with the House Director to enforce the house rules. She assigned rooms to the incoming girls in the fall, and parking places to individuals who found it necessary to have a car. These assignments were given on a point system. Points were made by holding a scholastic average, philanthropy, holding an office, attendance at meetings, etc., the ones with the highest points could select the best rooms and parking spots. The office of House Manager was a very difficult one, as she tried to remain part of the sisterhood in the house at the same time having the authority to enforce the rules. A very delicate balance.

The next officer was the Treasurer. She handled all incoming monies from rent, dues, and fees. The Vice President of Finance wrote all the checks for salaries, and house expenses, and handled the budgets for all of the activities during the year.

There were three Rush Chairs, two Internal and one External. I wrote in another chapter about "Rush" and the difficulty of this job.

Women in and out of the house also chaired the following positions. Social Chair, Risk Management, Philanthropy, Reference, Mentorship, Music and Continuing Education Chairs, and Chaplain.

All of the above were elected some time in November each year and took office in January. They then served for one year. Some officers were excellent and already had skill in their particular area. Others floundered through — sometimes gaining experience they could use later.

* * *

To my mind, the Treasurers had the most difficult jobs: developing budgets and funding the many activities during their terms. Some of the monies paid out were as follows:

The staff payroll, consisting of raises each year and a bonus at Christmas, was substantial. The food budget had to be enormous to feed over sixty women and a staff of ten, two full meals a day. The electric light bills and the gas for heating were overwhelming.

In addition to those expenses we had snow removal in the winter and lawn care during the summer, plus the underground sprinkling system. Carpet (mat rental service, for in front of the outside doors that were changed each month) knife sharpening service, trash pickup, and general maintenance were all considerable expenses.

Keeping the house in light bulbs, paper towels, toilet paper, foil and plastic bags of all sizes, trash bags, and other paper products was expensive. Then we had bottled water, a juice machine, coffee machines, coke machines, and washers and dryers to keep in running order. Fire extinguishers had to be checked and filled yearly; exit and emergency lighting had to be kept up to date. The security system had to be used properly and checked often. The sorority paid all of these expenses.

The exit lights were especially troublesome because they would shine in the girls' faces at night while they were trying to sleep, but of course, they were necessary. So the women would find ways to make it work for them by putting towels over the lights or taking out the bulbs. Our houseman would then replace the bulbs and remove the towels each time. We also had yearly inspections for the exits.

Money for new roofs, boilers, carpeting, painting, papering, plastering, all remodeling, and new furniture was furnished by the House Corporation Board. They owned the house and rented it to the sorority for a monthly fee. During the summer the Board would repaper seven or eight bedrooms, replace carpets in four or five rooms, and furnish requests by the women for additional lighting, computer outlets in each bedroom, and cable TV.

Hardly a week went by without an emergency of some sort: leaks in the ceiling from overflowing toilets or showers, doors, locks, windows broken or equipment breaking down. We had two vacuums for the girls' use. The vacuums needed constant attention. We found many strange things sucked up into them such as socks, pins, paper, and make-up; and the bags were so full the vacuums were putting out more than they were picking up. Some of the women cleaned their bedrooms regularly; some only when they were expecting their parents or their rooms were going to be inspected by the House Corp. That's when everything in sight went up into the vacuums, and they would begin to smoke or just die.

Mrs. W.

I just wanted to say thank you so much for the lovely card and the linen spray. What a generous gift! I really appreciate your kindness and I feel as if it is you who deserves the present. Thank you for being so understanding and flexible with all the changing rush plans. You were such a wonderful person to work with and I appreciate everything. Thank you again ..

♡always
Jara

Chapter 29

Rush was an activity that happened each fall when the new freshmen girls arrived on campus. They were wooed by all of the sororities, and the activities were well structured with many rules and regulations as to how this was done. Rush generally occurred early in September and lasted sometimes three to four weeks. The timeframe changed through the years, but the rules remained pretty much the same.

Rush was accomplished in four separate segments which were divided as follows:

First Sets, Second Sets, Third Sets, and Final Desserts.

The First Sets allowed all of the freshmen women to visit each sorority. They were divided into groups of around fifty and escorted to the houses. They remained inside about twenty minutes during which time they were entertained by the sorority women, given snacks, and had one-on-one conversations. There usually was a theme planned by the sorority, and the house decorated accordingly, and special dress was worn. In my house, the First Sets depicted a cozy atmosphere with the girls wearing pink pajamas, with teddy bears, stuffed animals, a bed made up of pink quilts, and the whole house looking very inviting. As the new girls waited outside to come in, the ones inside set up a roar by banging on the doors and windows or on pots and pans to gear themselves up for the occasion.

Then they sang some of their favorite Rush songs as the new people came in the door. The next 20 minutes were given over to talk and it sounded like thousands of bees buzzing as one hundred women got to know each other. Pretzels, nuts, and punch or water was served and after their twenty minutes were up they were ushered out with another song, and were led to the next sorority house to do the same thing over again, usually six or seven times during the first night.

First Sets were scheduled for two days so each group visited all of the sorority houses. Usually the sessions lasted four hours each day.

After the First Sets were over, the sorority women would gather to hash over what they thought of the new girls and they would keep notes on the favorable ones. These chosen women were invited back to what they called Second Sets.

For Second Sets, the whole process was repeated with a different theme and maybe different refreshments. In our house, half of the visitors were entertained with a skit, while the other half were given a tour of the girls' bedrooms. Of course, they all cleaned and vacuumed their rooms for the occasion. They, again, got to know the new women better by chatting and visiting. Time was a little longer to allow for better communications. Sometimes instead of a skit, they would work on a project of crafts, which they later delivered to the children's hospital or other organizations. They were again ushered in and out with singing.

Third Sets were a little more complicated. In my house, they performed a dance from a musical, and they were very good.

They had costumes and music and I marveled at their talent each year. I didn't know what the other houses did, but I'm sure they were equally as good.

So after each set the women would hash and eliminate and choose. This process went on well into the morning, especially after the third sets because they had to pare their lists down to approximately ninety women, or whatever number they were allotted.

These women were then invited to attend the Final Desserts. They were divided into three groups and would attend in formal attire. The women in my house all dressed in black, both short and long dresses. The dining room was fixed up in elegant fashion and a special dessert was served. On this occasion, I was introduced to each group as they finished eating. Then after each group left, tables had to be made up fresh for the next sitting. They again chatted like magpies with these girls to get some idea whether they would fit into our sorority. Hashing after Final Desserts became an all-night affair.

* * *

Each house had a quota for the number of women they could accept after Final D's. During the last years, the quota at my house was approximately forty new pledges. That meant that only about forty could be chosen out of about nine hundred to a thousand women who passed through the house.

Just as each house chose the women they wanted to have as sisters, the freshmen girls also had to state their first, second, and third choices of which house they wanted to join. The entire system was very complicated, but all of the choices on both sides went into a computer at the university. By noon of the following day, we found out the names of the women we chose, who had also chosen us, and there was generally an uproar as the lists were read. It seemed that each year the results were exactly what the women in my house expected. They were very good at Rush and always made their quota.

Some of the houses that didn't make their quota had a chance to have another Rush later in the year. Sometimes in that way they were able to get more members.

The same afternoon that the names were announced, the women in the house decorated their cars with balloons and streamers and went over to the dorms to pick up their new prospective members. They drove around campus tooting their horns for a while and then brought the new girls over for ice cream sundaes, or other planned activities.

* * *

That was the start of gradually introducing the new pledges into our house, making them feel at home, and keeping in touch with them until they moved into the house the following fall. They were invited to the house for dinner once a week, and encouraged to come over to study or "hang out" as the saying goes.

I really didn't get to know these new girls until they moved in. I already had over sixty living in, so to keep track of over one hundred was difficult. The girls I did get to know first generally were the officers, as I worked closely with them. Then there were the leaders who stood out, and of course, the troubled ones. Each year we had a number of each.

Usually around November the fifty new girls would come over with their sleeping bags to spend the night, and in the morning would be initiated into the sorority. The parents were notified when this would take place and almost all sent beautiful flowers. The ceremony was private and all wore white gowns, and candles were involved but more than that I can't attest to.

Except it was a very busy time for a very short while and everyone was very tired.

The next fall all of the new members, now sophomores, moved into the house and they, in their turn, went through Rush with the incoming freshman girls. The stress of arranging classes, buying books, moving into the house, taking part in Rush, and studying took its toll, and generally we had a lot of ailments: flu, coughing, and exhaustion. I feel tired just writing about it, but it was very exciting, and gratifying to get through.

12·20

Mrs. W.

Merry Christmas!! Thank you so much for all that you do. I know that many times we are busy & don't take the time to tell you how much we appreciate you & the things you do for us, but we do. I love the talks we have... I hope we can continue having them. Enjoy the holiday... I know you'll have a good time visiting w/ your family. Hopefully it will be a white christmas!!

Happy Holidays!

♡ Megan

Chapter 30

I should describe here the wonderful things that the House Corporation Board did for the house. They owned the house and the girls paid rent to live there. The Board was made up of officers, like any other corporation, and each and every one of the women who volunteered their services was a caring and capable person. They met at the house four times during the year to discuss finances and plan what improvements or repairs would take place during the summer months when the girls were gone.

Some of the women had been serving on the board before I arrived on the scene and for many years before then. I attended their meetings and was asked for input as to how the house was doing, what the problems were and how could they be of help. They were wonderful and it made my job so much easier knowing they were there for me.

Besides the rent that the board received from the house, they were given donations by alumni who were very generous and took an interest in supporting the sorority. Sometimes the money was given for a specific project, like furnishing the study room, or a new clock for the mantle, or just to be used as seen fit.

In some sororities the Corporation Board hired the House Director. They gave her salary and regular job ratings and more or less decided whether to rehire her for the coming year. In my sorority, I was hired by the girls and their advisor. I was also paid by the girls in the house and they determined my raises and bonuses. We had one advisor as opposed to other houses having advisory boards. All of these were directives that came from the nationals. For instance, if I wanted to take a weekend off, I had to hire a house sitter to come in at night to be with the girls. That was a national rule. Other houses allowed the women to be alone over night.

Some of the women on our board had lived in the sorority house as students years before, some were from our sorority at other schools in other states. At any rate, I admired them very much and enjoyed working with them through the years.

The
W.
Returns!

Chapter 31

After Rush, the new pledges would come over for dinner. As I observed them, I would perceive a certain flavor in the group as a whole and would get a sense of the dynamic I would be facing the following year. There was a year (several back) when I sensed trouble. A certain attitude existed that was a very pronounced warning that behavior had taken a step in the wrong direction. The "ME" concept was very strong and as I look back I can see it had been leading up the "I want it now, and don't tell me I can't have it" syndrome.

The manner of dress changed gradually to emulate boys and behavior changed in that direction as well. Baseball caps were worn backwards at meals, larger boots, tilting back chairs, feet up on tables, poor table manners, and loud vulgar language. Of course the change was not all at once, and certainly not all of the women. But enough to start me thinking of retirement for the second time. I was even told by the girls already living in the house, who had a hand in selecting these new people, that if I were going to retire, this was the time to do so.

I was torn, because most of my memories, in spite of the problems, had been of the wonderful, talented women who made my job so rewarding. But I felt I had to call it a day and turned in my resignation. I informed the Board and they expressed their disappointment, but they honored my decision, and interviewing for a new House Director began.

A new House Director was usually decided upon in March or April so that the house was assured of opening on time. I was not asked to sit in, and although I did meet some of the candidates, I did not express my opinion, even though I had some strong reactions. But of course I had to let go and prepare for my departure. I was given a surprise luncheon and they invited my family, so it was a very friendly send-off.

*   *   *

I left around the first of May, and as I usually had the summer off, it wasn't too different than the other years. But in the fall, I received a call from another sorority three days before school was to start. They were unable to hire a House Director, still didn't have a cook, and would I please come in and lend a hand. After the summer I was usually happy to return to work, and I did feel badly for them. So I said, "Yes," and found myself right back in the world of women and all of their problems, but in another setting.

I couldn't be too particular because of the time limit, but I was fortunate to find a cook, and then I moved in to familiarize myself with the new house and new women. The house itself was not kept up as my previous one had been, and many things went wrong immediately. The kitchen and dining room were in the basement with no windows, which seemed very strange.

If I thought my first quarters, when I started many years ago, were small and cramped — these were much more so. My living room, although on the first floor, had no windows, but had a stove, refrigerator, and sink. That took up much of the room so there was only space left for a very small couch and chair. The bedroom was smaller but at least had a window and the bathroom was the best of the three.

This sorority did not have a local House Corp. so everything had to be dealt with long distance. This slowed progress and I had to talk to many different people to have repairs completed. I was used to handling all this myself, so found it difficult. Throughout all of these initial situations, I found myself saying, "This is only temporary." Otherwise, I would have become very discouraged. When they hired me it was for just the first semester so I had only four months to go.

As I have stated before, the girls seem to perpetuate themselves when they choose new members so these women were entirely different than those I was used to. They didn't seem to need me at all. All of their events were planned and executed before I knew what was happening. They were very self-sufficient in many ways. I was used to planning with the women when they had activities, handling a lot of problems, and having personal chats with them when they felt the need. This was so different I felt rather that I had lost control and this was not a good feeling. When you are the director of something and that feeling of being in control is not there, it is quite uncomfortable.

The rest of the staff were in place so we got along fine for the four months. Then it was time for me to move on again.

* * *

I spent the summer as usual playing some golf, dancing, painting, etc., and as it passed I thought more and more how much I missed my old house, the girls, and the hustle and bustle of each day. Along about July I became aware that I wanted to go back to being a Director. I missed that good feeling of having contributed something to someone — a feeling of accomplishment at the end of the day. So once again I resurrected and updated my resume and sent it back hoping to find a house in need of a director.

In the meantime, I had heard rumors that the woman who had replaced me when I retired was not working out and would not be returning the following year. I wanted so badly to return to that place where I had spent seven or eight years, but I would have taken another house if need be. I was so happy when they called and asked for an interview and just knew I would be back again where I wanted to be.

While I was away there had been a lot of discord between the girls, the staff, and the House Director. The rumor was that the girls had signed a petition to get her out, and the staff had all threatened to quit. So when I met with them in the fall to prepare to open the house, they welcomed me back with open arms and I felt wonderful. They had hired a cook's helper while I was gone and she said, "I don't even know you, and I'm glad your back." The hugs I got were wonderful.

It was a great ego trip. As more years went by there were still many times, as on any job, when retirement seemed desirable, but there were also many great moments, and wonderful notes from the girls, about how they appreciated what I did for them and the house. That made it all worth while.

LUNCH WILL BE DELAYED

UNTIL ALL LUGGAGE &
BOXES ARE REMOVED
FROM THE UPSTAIRS HALL

FIRE HAZZARD !
tks.   W

Chapter 32

Each spring when I closed the house I had a different experience. Anywhere from fifteen to twenty-five women would be moving into apartments or houses and couldn't take occupancy until sometimes a week or more after the house closed. Group by group, they would come to me with this or that sad story and ask, or rather beg, to remain in the house longer. They didn't want to have to move their mountains of clothes and things twice and didn't have any place to stay until they could move into the new quarters.

My eight plus months of living with these girls had usually taken its toll, and I was more than anxious to have them gone. I loved most of them dearly, but enough was enough. But of course, being the pushover that I was, I would set down some rules but end up allowing them to stay. Each time I did, I regretted it because they took advantage of my leniency and instead of quietly spending time here waiting, they spent their time partying. I would see them in the TV room watching their favorite movies and remind them that: "Shouldn't they be up packing so when the time came they would be ready?" They informed me that they would be, not to worry.

I worried. Each time I took them at their word, and each time their word meant nothing, it was only given to keep me quiet.

Sometimes I heard them moving out at midnight, bumping huge trunks down the stairs. Sometimes they were entertaining in their rooms, against another rule I had made. I always found the doors left open because after they loaded their cars they would get in and leave. Anyone or anything could have wandered in. The peace and quiet I was much in need of was always postponed and I felt betrayed.

Each time I would vow that next year I would do it differently — even saying so to the girls as they left. But most of them weren't coming back anyway so what did they care. You know of course that by the time the next house closing came around I repeated my mistake and let them talk me into it again. This happened many years in a row, but each time I thought that surely these new women wouldn't do the same thing. They were different weren't they? More mature? No they weren't, they were just more polite about it.

I did learn a little. One year I told them they could leave their belongings but they had to be out on a certain day. They would be allowed back at a certain time to pick up their things, and the move out shouldn't take too long. They had promised that they would be ready to move out when they returned. I didn't learn until too late that they hadn't even started to pack and would take days to clear all of the stuff out of their rooms. After that they were supposed to clean, vacuum and dust. Very few did this.

So I learned a little more. The next time the house was closing, I let them leave their things, but they had to be all packed with everything they owned downstairs in the living room ready to go. Their rooms had to be empty and clean before they left on the last day. This actually worked until they came back for the stuff. Four were coming back on a Monday, three on a Tuesday, five on Wednesday, four the following Sunday, and at a set time each day. Some of them did come on time, some were late, and something that I hadn't counted on, they had to make several trips back and forth to take their clothes, TV's, computers, shelves, bookcases, irons, cosmetics, bedding, towels, books, fans, and all of their personal things. These things filled three very large rooms in our downstairs.

Some of them didn't show up when they had promised they would and I didn't have phone numbers yet so couldn't call. If I were lucky I would spot them walking to their classes, which had started, and would chase them down.

I moved to another place in the summer, so even though I had to stay for a week or so to make sure the house was secure, cancel the trash pickup, get the sprinkler system going — and many other tasks — I didn't let the girls know that. I made them believe I had to come back each day to meet them and let them in. No one except the people who worked in the house in the summer were allowed to have a key. On their last day in the house, I had the locks changed on all three outside doors, so even if they didn't turn in their keys they could not get in. And if they didn't turn in their keys they didn't get their key deposit back.

So when I hugged and said goodbye to the last girl, I finally had the quiet I was waiting for. After the voices (eighteen and nineteen year old girls have very high pitched, carrying ones), and the loud music, the stomping around upstairs, and up and down the stairs, the doors slamming all over the house, the dishes and pans clanging, the questions and problems, no one could imagine what that silence did for me. If I hadn't had that restful and quiet time for the balance of the summer, I never could have returned. But somehow at the end of summer, I was really looking forward once again to taking care of about fifteen returning women from the year before, and forty-five new ones.

The staff and I would find out anew their tastes in food, music, entertainment, dress, manners, and their many personalities. It was always an interesting mix and there were always surprises, some good and some bad. But that was ok. And I learned something very valuable each year that passed about everything.

Mrs. W,

I want to wish you a very happy birthday on this special day! I truly appreciate all you do for me ~ as well as for the house. Thank you for all of the times you have been there for me to encourage me, help me, and just listen to me babble. You really are my house mom! Once again, thank you, and have an _amazing_ birthday!

♡, amy R.

p.s. Here is a little gift for you to use for the little notes you write! I am looking forward to working with you next semester!

Chapter 33

Throughout the years, certain women stood out, or interacted more readily with me. A few lived in the house for three years, which allowed for a deeper relationship. Somehow the troubled ones always stood out in your mind, with the hope that things would turn out well. Here are a few personalities from the three sororities that I was fortunate enough to live in.

MARY:

She was like no other girl through the years. Half woman and half little girl, she needed a lot of caring and guidance. I think really that morally she was better than average, but liked to talk otherwise. She would be gone from the house frequently and I would miss seeing her around. When questioned she told me that she had a bed in a fraternity and sometimes spent her nights there. I guess I was surprised because I hadn't heard that one before. Having been inside of a fraternity house, it was hard for me to believe that the girls could eat and party there — let alone sleep there. It felt all wrong to me, but she told me in such a matter-of-fact way, that it somehow seemed innocent.

SUE:

This girl had more money than she could be responsible for. Her checkbook and wallet were continually left in the public rooms in the house. She actually loaned out her credit cards. And whenever I heard loud, foul language it was generally her. She lived in the same city as the sorority but was generally the last to return to her home and the first one back after breaks. So my breaks from her were shortened and that wasn't something I desired.

CARRIE:

She kept me on my toes for nearly two years. Everything that was not supposed to be done, Carrie would do. It seemed that when anything was wrong in the house, eventually it ended up at her door. I would try very hard to be friends with her, and on a one-on-one basis she could be very charming, but then she would be heard saying some outrageous thing or doing some ridiculous thing and we would be back to square one. She did not have a parking spot but was continually using someone else's, which caused havoc in the lot.

CAITLIN:

She was delightful. Vivacious, smart, cute, and she had a voice that carried all through the house. Continually losing her belongings, leaving her keys in her car, locked. Someone broke into her car when it was parked right in our driveway, and of course half of her belongings were in there along with her wallet. Her mother came often to help straighten out her problems and her only comment, always, was, "That's Caitlin."

SARAH AND SALLE:

Identical twins. Very smart, beautiful girls and one was elected to be the House Manager one year. As I mentioned in the story the House Manager and I worked very closely together to enforce the rules of the house and she was the go-between for me at the chapter meetings. We would meet before chapter and I could express to her things that I needed to change or improve about the house. It was very difficult because each time I would approach one of the twins, thinking that I had the one I needed to talk to, it would be the wrong one. It became embarrassing and I needed some way to tell the difference. So they told me a secret…only one of them had her ears pierced. So I would carefully lift aside the long blond hair to verify my twin. Problem solved. They both kept a four point average and were wonderful to have around.

PENNY:

The sweetest girl I have ever met. Out-going, sincere, and completely herself, she graced our house with smiles and charm. She had studied ballet in New York and was interested in everyone and everything. Her speech was accompanied by wide gestures and expressions when relating events that could only have happened to her. She explained to me in a wonderfully breathless way, along with hand movements that she was going to drive to her home several hours away, but had never driven on the expressway before. She expressed no fear, only excitement, but I was very worried for I didn't want anything to ever happen to Penny that wasn't good. She made it home and back many times but I always worried.

MARIA:

Tall, dark — like an Indian princess. During her last year here, she had the misfortune of loosing her hair. I know her family took her everywhere to find help, but somehow even after it came back in, it fell out again. But we all had to admire her so, because she stood tall, and continued her life and studies in spite of her handicap. She did wear a wig occasionally but sometimes just appeared with it in tufts and spaces and showed the confidence we all envied. Considering how particular the college women are about their appearance — the need to be slim, have long beautiful hair, perfect teeth, smooth skin, etc. — she was a wonderful example of how to just be with what she had. We all admired her very much.

ANNE MARIE:

A very small package, actually shorter than me, (and I liked girls shorter so I could look them in the eye) and a ball of fire. She had charge of Rush one year and dictated to me, in no uncertain terms, just how she was going to do it. We had eight large tables in our dining room, but these were not suitable for Anne Marie, so she rented twelve more. When I inquired where she was going to store the eight, she said, "I'll put them somewhere even if I have to move them myself." And she could have. She did a great job and had my admiration as long as she was here.

ALICE:

Alice had a physical problem with her spine and had had surgery for the problem. But it didn't ever seem to heal. I accompanied her to the health service many times but other than dispensing pills for pain, they didn't seem to do much. She was so brave during all of this and kept her studies and social obligations up in spite of the situation. I knew her for probably three years and finally found out that her problem was taken care of during her visits home. I still think about her and all she went through.

CAROLYN:

She came to me about a month after move-in and expressed her unhappiness with nearly everything in the house. Her room, her roommate, the house, etc., and wanted to move out. She had friends who had remained in the dorms and she felt that she would have been much happier there. I tried to impress on her that if she moved or changed things every time it wasn't to her liking, she would find it hard out into the business world. Jobs are always good and bad, situations always carry problems, and maybe she should give it a little longer and try to be more positive and see what would happen. I found her later and asked how things were. She had decided to stay, and as I learned had planned to return next year. I was happy she stuck it out, for her sake.

LENORE:

This girl was a perfectionist. Played the piano beautifully, had a 4.0 average gradepoint, was going to be a lawyer, and was always studying. However, she did have an eating disorder and was equally as perfect at hiding it. She would come down before anyone else was awake and fill her backpack with bagels, or any other food that was available, but was hardly ever seen at the dinner table. She was very likable, but kept to herself, quietly did her schoolwork and was very responsible. I think being the only child, and the future lawyer of the family, put too much pressure on her success and may have caused the unnatural eating habits. Somehow, I know she will do her parents proud.

SIERRA:

Tall, lovely, and very troubled. Her moods were always fluctuating. Problems with boy friends, with roommates. One night she was simply screaming in her room and without my knowledge her sisters called the police. The girls were afraid she would hurt herself, I guess she had mentioned it, so the police told the girls that one or both of them should stay with her until morning and then maybe call her parents. She seemed better for a while after that, but eventually left in the middle of a semester. I later heard she was fine and was attending another school.

MEG:

This girl was very intelligent, but totally clueless about other things. One of the rules in the house was that wherever food was served shoes or socks must be worn at all times. I continually found Meg in the small kitchen in her bare feet. I had to keep reminding her that it was a health rule and must be kept. I couldn't believe my eyes one day when I found her again sitting at the table in the busboy's kitchen without either shoes or socks. I could see her from where I was in the big kitchen so when she looked at me I just pointed to her feet. She quickly pulled them up underneath her and said to me, "But Mrs. W. I'm not eating." Somehow because the rule was connected to the kitchen and dining room, she must have thought that it was ok not to cover your feet if you weren't eating. I just shook my head in wonder. I'm sure she wasn't thinking, and had just been caught off guard.

CORA:

She was not the skinny, size 0 or 2 figure that graced most of the girls in the house. Some had figures that were almost straight up and down. But she was comfortably plump (as one friend of mine called it, 'rounded') and was so completely comfortable and at ease with herself that you had to admire her. She wore the same clothes as the small girls and let it all hang out. With all of the eating disorders I have dealt with through the years, and with the thin image of the college girls in all of the magazines and television programs, I thought she was magnificent in her confidence and complete ability to be herself. To me, her image was healthy and wonderful but she was a rarity. Too bad.

DONNA:

This young woman was in charge of philanthropy one year and did an excellent job of facilitating projects that would bring joy to either young children in the hospitals around here, or for organizing gifts that were made by the girls and sent to St. Jude's Hospital. It took time and lots of effort and was done efficiently, but somehow, after being constructed, her projects didn't get delivered to the intended places for months. I had to keep reminding her that her projects were still downstairs in the basement, and inquire why they weren't shipped out or taken somewhere. She had charge of another project during her stay here, where money was collected. I had this pail of money in my bedroom for weeks and weeks before she finally did something with it. What makes this so outstanding in my mind is that she was also running for office at Panhel, and I attended to support her. Each candidate had two people who advocated on their behalf and explained why they should hold this office. The supporters were throwing around platitudes attributed to her, such as: 'responsible', 'organized', 'always ready to do and complete any job, as busy as she was with school'… I wasn't sure I was in the right place, and they were talking about the same girl I knew. At any rate, she was elected and as most of her responsibility for this office didn't affect the house or me, I will never know how she handled the job.

WHATEVER HAPPENED
IN THIS BATHTUB.....
THE STAFF REFUSES
TO CLEAN IT UP !!

                TKS. .W.

PLEASE DO
NOT LEAVE YOUR
DISHES IN THE
BATHROOMS.
WE DON·T HAVE PERSONAL
MAID SERVICE HERE... TKS
        .W.

Chapter 34

It's not uncommon to see the women in the house:

* Take the ties from their ponytails, shake their hair near the buffet table or over the salad bar and tie up their hair again.

* Put their feet up on any table within their reach with no regard for the cleanliness of their shoes.

* Drop food on the floor and walk on it. Do they do this at home?

* Put an empty coffee pot on a burner, turn on the burner and expect it to make coffee; I'm sure they had studying or partying on their minds.

* Leave their personal belongings in the public areas for days, and wonder why they can't find them later.

* Leave the toilets unflushed, the sinks full of hair, and enough eyebrow pencil shavings to block the drains.

* Pour soup or other food into the kitchen sink that does not have a disposal, leaving someone else to dig out the food.

* Iron clothes on the rug in their bedroom and burn a hole in the carpet.

* Turn on the TV and leave the room, just to have the noise. They seem to study better with that distraction.

* Pick at the food on the salad bar with their fingers and ignore the utensils that are provided.

* Take a bite of a sandwich, cupcake, apple, and put it back in the bowl. Maybe they think that is not being wasteful?

* Take the last cup of coffee and not turn off the burner.

* Vomit in the toilet, on the floor along side, or in the sinks or showers and leave it for someone else to clean.

* Use the doors that are on the alarm system after eleven P.M. and set it off, time after time.

* Leave their clothes in the washers and dryers for hours or days, or on top of the machines until they dry out and turn yellow.

* Almost never clean out the vent in the dryers after use.

* Prop open the outside doors to pack their cars when leaving for a weekend, or a break, and drive away without closing them, even late at night.

* Park in the middle of the driveway, come in the house and disappear, requiring that anyone wanting to get out of the parking lot will have to hunt them down.

* Collect enough unpaid parking tickets on the cars so that the city has to tow them away.

* Leave check books, credit cards, and money on tables and sofas — and not miss them for days.

* Leave cameras and other valuables in my possession for months before they think to look for them.

* Giggle and laugh much more than usual when there is a male dinner guest present.

* Borrow the house vacuums and leave them in their bedrooms so we have to search the rooms to find them.

* Come down to lunch in short pajamas, fuzzy animal slippers, hair uncombed, eyes barely open, and feel right at home even with guests present.

* Eat off the tops of muffins, the frosting from cakes, or any other toppings on desserts.

* Subscribe to newspapers, and when they arrive, ignore them until someone else picks them up and brings them in. There were sometimes eight or nine subscriptions at one time.

* Throw their cigarettes on the steps, grind them out with their shoe and leave ugly black marks, ignoring the containers.

* Come in at three A.M. and slam the doors to their rooms, the bathrooms, and the dormers at least three times each before settling in.

* Leave the bright lights on all over the house when they leave or retire, yet sit at the dining room table in the dark, if someone else hasn't turned the lights on. I have observed girls studying in the dining room and when I turned on the light, they looked up so surprised —like they hadn't known that there lights there.

These are just a few of the trends that I observed during my days and nights in all three sororities. These things are amusing to write about, and I would guess quite universal in the college world.

Chapter 35

I entered this world of sororities as a House Mother, and, as the title implies, was invited into the lives of the girls over and beyond their studies and my official duties to look after their health and safety. They talked to me about emotional problems, their dating, breaking up and making up problems, their difficulty living with certain roommates, their inability to be happy away from home and family, their difficulty with certain foods, and many other small details that they encountered in their lives here.

When I became House Director things changed in a very slow and strange way. My job became like that of the manager of a small hotel. I still hired and supervised the staff, made out the menus, was responsible if the meals were not to their liking, tried to see that the rules of the house were kept, made sure things were fixed when broken, tried to keep people happy with the heat and/or cold in the bedrooms — just as I had done as a House Mother. But the more intimate problems seemed not to exist, or they were handled with peers, or not handled at all.

Recently the name 'Facilitator' has been hinted at and talked about by other women running sorority houses. I heard that in a short time that is what we might be called and to me it means that any lasting personal contact with the women could be named right of existence. Our supervision would take on a cold, arms-length attitude and whatever experiences we would have had to pass on to these young people would not be accepted. I'm not sure who came up with this title, but it has to be the Greek System, as they run the houses on campus. I sincerely hope that I am wrong about this name change and hope it never occurs, but we will have to wait and see.

I guess what I mean is that I hope to be gone when, and if, that happens. I want to remember the many young women who poured out their hearts to me, and I like to think that I helped the immediate problem in some small way. They were all so young and vulnerable, and some so far from home, without the solving ways of their immediate families. I want to remember those years with those young women, not the years after they discovered they could get whatever they wanted, when and how they wanted it, and "No" was unacceptable to them. I will always remember and cherish the former.

Dear Mrs. W,

I just wanted to thank you for everything you did this weekend to help out. I couldn't have pulled it off without you. It was a sure relief to a stressful weekend to work with someone to know how everything runs. We will be at a loss next year without you. Thanks again for everything.

Very truly yours,

Katie

P.S. I know you didn't get a chance to make a "pen, so this one is for you. :)

Chapter 36

More and more as the days and weeks pass, when confronted with a flooded floor at three in the morning, or blown fuses, or waking up to find that pictures and lamps have disappeared, I am really convinced that it is time for me to seek a more quiet place to live and a less stressful pace of life.

There is a tightness in my stomach that happens whenever anyone is ill, or when anyone knocks on my bedroom door at night for help. Most of the time through the years, I was able to take whatever went on in stride, and was able to return to sleep. Now, however, my body and nerves are not as resilient and sleep eludes me for the rest of the night.

But I still have this year to manage and with a great staff, I will give it my all.

* * *

I am so pleased to write about something that happened last week. I was visited by an advisor to a Fraternity called Delta Chi. They had been out of the Greek system for a time and were returning to their chapter hoping to recruit new members. One of them indicated to me that they had only nine at the present time, with a few leaning toward joining, and as some of the nine knew a few of my girls, would it be possible to come to dinner? They admired the women and liked the house, so of course I said I would love to have them. Nine more for dinner here is hardly a problem.

He went on to say that they hoped to be known as the "gentlemen" fraternity and that cinched it for me. I would have them every week for dinner if they could really be that, and maybe start a trend here on campus to go in that direction. They already had shirts printed with "gentlemen's fraternity" on the back. They presented one to me and I shall keep it with all of my other memorable things.

So a few days later two of the members of the fraternity came to visit me and we set a date for dinner. They were very polite and seemed excited about our upcoming dinner. We talked some more about presenting a nobler side of young men and how pleased I am with the prospect. So we set a date for Monday night, and they were going to come ten minutes early to visit with me before dinner.

They arrived — all in shirts, ties, and suits, all carrying either a few flowers or a pansy plant as their contribution to the event. Pansy is the flower for our sorority so that took some thinking on their part. The girls in the house who knew them came forward and I left them to visit while I helped the cook set out dinner. The busboy who was scheduled to do that did not show up. Just one of the stomach tighteners. No-shows on the busboy's part meant I needed to help the cook, who really depended on their services. This doesn't happen often as we usually have very dependable boys working in our kitchens.

I had printed place cards and seated the guests around the dining room at different tables with the girls, so they could get to know each other. It worked well. I had informed the gentlemen before dinner that I wouldn't be eating with them. I explained that I didn't usually eat with the girls. It is very noisy in the dining room and quite difficult to converse anyway. I'm sure the girls might like to talk about what they did the night before, and it might not be something I should hear so I take my dinner to a quiet place to enjoy. So I settled everyone and left them to get acquainted. I later went in to say goodnight and they all thanked me profusely. I think we all felt we had done something worthwhile.

I told the boys they would now be our champions and come to our aid in difficulties. They agreed, although their house is quite a distance from ours. But I couldn't help feeling that this very positive step could maybe bring about a few small changes that might grow into something bigger and permanent. Throughout the years I have lost respect for the sort of young men who break into our house time after time and create havoc. Hopefully in my final year here I can change that image, and really believe that 'the resurgence of gentlemanly behavior' is possible.

* * *

Another positive at this writing is the general behavior of the new women who moved into the house this fall. They are polite, respectful, and much less demanding than usual. Of course, you have to understand that every year the great majority of the girls are wonderful, and many go on to have great careers and lives. But the overall atmosphere of this group of girls is a great change, and a very positive one, from the past few years. So it should be a pleasant year and a calming one on my midsection.

I feel very tentative about finalizing my time here with these bright, promising, young women, but I am reassured and hopeful that their futures will be as bright as they are. I feel that I have witnessed so many aspects of their lives and experiences. They live in wonderful, but trying, times and the world will have high expectations of them.

* * *

Over the years, I have sometimes been Director, sometimes Mother, Advisor, Problem-Solver, Negotiator, Soother, Good Listener — and very often a little crazy. Many days were hectic, many were serene — but none of them ever dull. I guess that's why I stayed as long as I did. After living in this environment for so many years, I will definitely miss it. Also, the appreciation expressed by most of the women and the staff have made it all worthwhile.

My hopes and prayers go with these young people, to wherever they are destined, and they will always have a special place in my heart.

Postscript

My four grandchildren grew up spending a lot of time in the sorority house. They are all teenagers now, but when they were little this was a haven when they were home from school for various illnesses. That way their mothers could go to work and I welcomed the chance to be with them on a one-on-one basis. Usually they recovered very quickly with tender loving care, chicken soup (and almost anything they could want in the food line as our pantry was always full of good food) and, of course, the attention of myself and the staff. Their mothers would pick them up at the end of the day and we all benefited from the visit. It was tempting for them to be sick just to come to my house, and I would have been just as happy to see them.

When the younger granddaughter was about four or five, and we were having lunch one day, a busboy picked her up from behind and swung her up in the air. She really didn't like that and the next time we were scheduled to have lunch at the house, she wanted to know if the "boy busses" were going to be there. I assured her that they would not play that trick again, as she wanted no more of that.

My entire family enjoyed many very special occasions at the

sorority. With such a large house and a fully equipped kitchen, many times we had our Thanksgiving dinners there. At Christmas, the girls put up a very large, tall tree that extended up into the circular stairway and each decorated an ornament with glitter and their name and year. So my family and I celebrated Christmas Eve there and sometimes Christmas Day. All of the women went home for the holidays so we had the house completely to ourselves.

As I mentioned above, we had a beautiful winding staircase that rose to the third floor, so we played a game of throwing pennies down into a hat, to see who had the best aim. And it was a wonderful place to play hide and seek, with over forty rooms on four floors. There was a flat roof on the back of the house and we could go up there and watch the parties in progress next door, or drop things onto a target below. They loved to spend the weekend and occupy the two couches in my living room at night watching TV and getting into the snacks that were plentiful in my closets. The girls wanted to be House Directors when they grew up because they thought all I had to do was entertain them, and the staff did all the work. Outwardly it might have seemed that way.

In this large house, it was easier to find the children than it was to find the staff sometimes. If the maid or houseman received an important phone call someone had to search for them as their duties took them throughout the house. A scary thought, almost always with me, was how easy it would be for a stranger to gain entrance and hide in the house. I imagine anyone could move from room to room and not be found for days. I was continually reminding the girls to please make sure the doors were closed and worried about it when I was away from the house.

The following writings are from my grandchildren who very generously agreed to share their experiences of the sorority houses where I spent so many years:

For as long as I can remember, my Nana has lived in a sorority house. When I was younger, I always thought about what a great job she had, and that I wanted to be a director when I grew up. Every morning, all she had to do to get to work was walk down the hallway. What job could be better? It would be many years before I would come to realize that she did much more than to simply wake up and walk down the hallway everyday. I use to wonder how long Nana would work at the sorority house. I can remember asking her that question many times, and telling her how funny it would be if she still worked there when I was in college. She would laugh and tell me that that would never happen. I laugh now though because here I am finishing my sixth year of college and graduating just as she is finishing her career. I knew it would happen!

Throughout the years I liked taking my friends to see Nana's house. They were amazed and couldn't believe the 'mansion' she lived in. Even now, when I tell my friends about the sorority house, they are interested in what goes on there, and what a House Director actually does. In the summertime, all of us kids could run all through the house hiding and jumping out at each other. One time, my sister and I were hiding from each other and we didn't know Nana was even upstairs. She hid around a corner and jumped out at us as we ran by. That was definitely an unexpected scare, and not to mention, the start of a brand new game.

When classes ended in April and the girls moved out, Nana would let my sister and I go through the rooms looking for pennies that had been left. Some years we left there with quite a few of them. One thing I will always remember is helping Nana bring up the cereal for the week. She would say "let's load this onto the dumb waiter, and pull it upstairs, so we don't have to carry it." I had no idea that that was what it was actually called until I was older. I learned so much at that house.

As I mentioned before, it would take years for me to discover just how much Nana did at her job every day. Two years ago, I began being the substitute House Director when Nana went on vacation. There has to be someone in charge there every night, and since I am finally old enough, and I knew the house so well, I was that person. It was not easy being 'in charge' of what goes on in a house full of my peers. However, that was not a problem in comparison to the seven-out-of-nine nights I was there when the burglar alarm went off. During the middle of the night was when I really began to see how much Nana did on her job. It is not just a nine-to-five job; it's a twenty-four-hour a day, and seven-days a week job. The weeks I spent being the House Director were definitely more work than I had planned on, but they were fun and enlightening. I no longer say that Nana has had an 'easy' job for the past 18 years.

I think that of all my memories of the sorority house, my favorite are those of the Christmas Eves we spent there. The whole family would come to the house to celebrate and every year Nana would have to remind all of the grandchildren not to run inside. This final year, though, Nana hid our presents all throughout the house. She gave each of us a clue to help us find them. She made it a race, and told us that the first one to find their gift and come back to the Christmas tree won the prize. She even let us run.

This sorority house has been like my own home for all those years. I never thought I would grow so attached to it. The thought of not being able to just stop by the house anymore is very sad. It is where I learned how to play the piano, where I did countless homework assignments, where Nana and I play hopscotch on the sunroof during the summers, and where we shared so much fun and laughter. The sorority house may be very large and sometimes makes strange noises, but for me it has and will always be a very safe, comfortable and wonderful place.

Krista

It's hard to remember everything you experienced as a child, especially since things went by so fast. But there are those certain people, and certain places that are etched in your mind so deeply, you could swear they happened yesterday. Memories that you refuse to forget because reliving them is like your own private dessert, which you can dive into without guilt. That's why my time in this sorority, and with my Nana, has meant so much to me. Although not too many people had the opportunity to grow up and experience adolescence in a house like this, it wasn't too much different than your typical childhood, with a few perks. Well, for a boy, maybe a little more. However, the house full of girls didn't exceed the mystery, size, and warmth the sorority provided on its own.

You don't truly understand how important some places are to you until either you have to leave them or, in my case, drift away. Looking back, no matter how unconventional (which in no way means a bad thing) it might have been, it is where I grew up — from a young boy hiding beneath the stairs shy, yet curious of the girls who roamed the house; my cousins, along with my sister and I, playing hide and seek and pitching a small tent like we were somewhere unknown. That was where I would get my first job as a busboy, serving the girls who I once ran from. And that is also where we celebrated holidays.

Christmas was exciting and wonderful every year when the girls left, making the place ours. It's hard to imagine that my life has not been affected by this house and especially by my Nana, who basically made her work her home. This house is full of stories, truly good stories, and I hope you can find great enjoyment in them, as I have.

Casey

Ever since I was two years old I have been going to the sorority to visit my Nana. Some of the smallest things that have happened there are some of the biggest memories that I have.

Every time I felt sick and could not go to school, my mom would drop me off at the sorority. I was always taken very good care of while I was there. I would get all of the soup that I needed! Somehow, by the time I would leave the sorority, I was always feeling just fine.

When I was younger, I thought that my Nana's job at the sorority was so easy. No matter how many times people told me everything that she did, I did not believe them, because when I was visiting, she would sit in the living room with me and watch T. V. Plus, she didn't have to go outside to get to work, her apartment was only about 100 feet from her work. I found that amazing. It turns out that she does do so much more than just sit around eating crackers and peanut butter and drinking hot chocolate. I still believe that being a House Mother is the best job a person could have.

There have been so many years that we celebrated Christmas Eve at the sorority. During dinner we would all scratch off the lotto tickets that Nana put by our plates. I don't think I ever actually won though. Soon after dinner we would open presents, and there would be envelopes for each of the grand-children on the tree. Inside were rhymes / hints to where our presents could be found. Nana hid them all over the house. It was always so much fun when the whole family got together at the sorority house.

When the girls left for summer vacation, my sister and I would race into every bedroom to collect the money they had left behind. Usually, it would be in the dresser drawers or in the closets, on the floor. We only found pennies, and nickels, but we would get so excited over that. Sometimes, I would find teddy bears or even clothes that I wanted. Nana would put everything we found in the lost and found. If it was not retrieved when the girls returned in the fall, then we got to keep them.

When the girls were gone I would go into the T. V. room and work on my gymnastics routines or make up dances. My cousin, Hallie, and I have made up many dances in the living room there. We loved it, because there was so much space. From ballet to jazz to hip-hop, we were always dancing. The era when we were obsessed with N SYNC was a good time. Every dance move to every song that they sang, we had memo-rized. Of course we had to perform every one of them for Nana. She loved watching us. She would even teach us some of the steps she knew from all of her dancing experience.

Going to the sorority for so many years was so much fun. In 2003, when I started college, I began to work there. I was one of the 'bus boys'. On Mondays, Thursdays, and Fridays I would help set-up and clean-up dinner. I did not mind the work at all, and it was only for a couple of hours a day. Plus, I would get dinner and I got to spend time with my Nana. The food there was unbelievable. A full dinner, salad bar, and dessert was always just what I needed. It helped a lot that everyone who worked there was so incredibly nice.

I wish that I could still say that I can't wait for next year to again visit the sorority, but I can't. Nana is retiring this year. Even though there will be no continuing memories, I will carry the ones that I do have forever.

For the past 16 years I have been visiting my Nana at the sorority. I am now eighteen years old. Since I can remember, that was where we visited, and shared so many stories, memories, and good laughs. There were also many of my problems talked about, in the same spot, in the same living room.

It just seemed that the sorority was the perfect place to go when I needed to relax, even though it could have been the most hectic. It is weird how that works out. So even though the time spent in the sorority is over, I am so happy that I had it, and I will miss it tremendously.

Jamie

Author Biography

Ms. Devine was born in the Upper Peninsula of Michigan. She lived in California and Tennessee and then moved to the Lower Peninsula in 1950, where her sons and grandchildren also reside. Her love of dance has kept her active and she currently continues to enjoy ballroom dancing. After a career in the advertising world, she became involved with house mothering and at this point is planning her retirement from this very challenging, but rewarding, position. She will continue to live in Michigan.